D1180234

Superintendent Harry King and Chief Inspector Owen were friends. Both worked at Scotland Yard in the anti-narcotics section.

Their wives were friendly too. The four played bridge and went out together socially, to parties, even to picnics. It was at one such picnic that a horrific misunderstanding took place which breached the friendship between the women.

A criminal called Buller whom King had had imprisoned, swore vengeance against King. Their paths unluckily crossed again when King, in retirement, was employed to protect a marriage bureau called Sure Friendship.

From that time the clash between Buller and King becomes inevitable; and in the event it takes a horrific and bloody form.

John Bingham is among the most distinguished suspense novelists writing today. From classics like *Five Roundabouts to Heaven* up to his recent brilliant *The Marriage Bureau Murders* he has set a standard admired throughout the world. His many followers will want to investigate the sinister world of *Deadly Picnic*.

DEADLY PICNIC

John Bingham

M

ISBN: 0 333 28487 9

First published 1980 by
MACMILLAN LONDON LIMITED
*4 Little Essex Street London WC2R 3LF
and Basingstoke
Associated companies in Delhi Dublin Hong Kong
Johannesburg Lagos Melbourne New York Singapore
and Tokyo*

Printed in Great Britain by
THE ANCHOR PRESS LTD
Tiptree, Essex

Bound in Great Britain by
WM BRENDON & SON LTD
Tiptree, Essex

CHAPTER ONE

Harry King and Bill Owen both worked in the Yard's anti-narcotics circus, as they called it.

King, in his late forties, was a superintendent; Owen, a few years younger, was a chief inspector. But the difference in rank had never made their conversation stilted nor interfered with their friendship and the easy badinage they indulged in now and again. Besides, it was generally understood that when King retired, as he intended to do in the not-too-distant future, Owen would take over his position – the Commissioner agreeing. At any rate, Harry King would press for it.

'Yes, you're right, they're coppers,' Madge Owen once told a stranger who had overheard them together at a party. 'But quite harmless.'

It was a lie, though she certainly didn't know how big a lie. Each in his way was as deadly as the other.

Outwardly, they were different. King was tall, leanly built, with a square face and jaw, and a big straight nose. His eyes were grey and his plentiful coarse dark hair had grey streaks. His short hair above the ears was also going grey. His complexion, especially in winter, tended to be grey, too. This was nothing to do with health, but was due to the colour of the skin with which he was born. He was an Anglo-Saxon type, in appearance and slowness of speech, but somewhere along the line there was, as with Owen, a Celtic strain, perhaps from Cornwall, which gave him an ability to think with subtlety and appreciate Owen's faster, more imaginative reactions.

People called King 'the pallid fox'.

Bill Owen was a very different animal. He was stocky, short for a police officer, with a thick thatch of black hair, brown eyes, a round face, a ruddy complexion, thick red lips and a snub nose. His Welsh father came from a county which had had the pretty name of Merioneth, until a Conservative government ceased to conserve it and it became Gwynedd. With his melodious voice and vivid imagination, Owen had inherited much of his father's character.

For his part, Bill Owen not only recognised the value of Harry King's solid, thorough methods. He admired his superior to a pitch which is unusual in such a down-to-earth profession – or in any other, for that matter. But then, there was a lot more in Owen than met the eye. Anybody's eye. For Owen had a secret. True, Harry King sometimes thought Owen's imagination too vivid. But not even he realised how far, or in what disparate directions, his colleague's mind ranged.

He would not have believed it if he had not been told.

The men's unexpected friendship was also greatly helped by the fact that their wives seemed to get on well together. One reason for that may have been that, like the men, they differed so much, physically and temperamentally.

As a partial counterbalance to her husband, Madge Owen came from the borders of Yorkshire and Lancashire and had a practical northern approach to life. She was tall, almost masculine in some ways, dark-haired and with dark button eyes, quick-witted – and quick-tempered.

Harry King's wife, Laura, was unlike any of them.

Perhaps that was why she was to cause such deadly upsets among them. Behind her tranquil, almost coy façade, she had a streak of unpredictability that was almost otherworldly. It would cause her to say and do strange things; as they were all to find out very soon.

Bound up with that, she had the capacity to evoke both intense love, and sometimes – hate. The two can be similar. In Harry King's case it was love; very much so. He loved her to distraction. He would have died for her. And, though he did not know it himself yet, he would have killed for her.

She was ten years younger than King; small, petite, slim about the waist, legs, ankles and wrists, she had fair, shoulder-length hair and a curiously tawny complexion.

Owen once said she had the lightest amber eyes he had ever seen in a woman – or in a man, come to that. Madge asked him quickly how many amber cat-like eyes he had looked into. He was tempted to turn the question lightly, but that imagination of which Harry King sometimes mildly disapproved enabled Owen to see what he conceived to be a tiny red danger signal at the end of a very long tunnel. He pursed his lips as he did when he tried to play the flute, which he sometimes did at the end of an evening, and his brown eyes twinkled.

'Lots! Some ended up on the gallows, though they wouldn't now. If they knock off a copper they give 'em a packet of fags and tell 'em to be good boys in future,' he added facetiously.

'Don't talk like that!' Madge had flared back. 'You know I don't like it, all that talk of coppers being knocked off. I won't have it, Bill Owen, I won't.'

The subject of eyes was forgotten, though for good measure he added: 'Nice lass, Laura, but she reads romantic novels. And poetry, and muck like that. Know what? Old Harry once told me she read poetry in bed on their honeymoon!'

Madge laughed. She thought her Bill would never fall for anybody who could read poetry in bed on a honeymoon.

Her mind was at rest, as Owen guessed it would be.

Chief Inspector Owen's imagination would sometimes take off in an unpredictable manner. On the afternoon they all went on the picnic, for instance, he lay peacefully on his side on the dry ground engaging in one of his more quirky trains of thought. He was wondering about guardian angels, he told Harry King.

What was the sex of a guardian angel? Was the standard guardian angel a he or a she? If it was a she, was is a Mrs, or a Ms? He came to the conclusion that, whether Women's Lib liked it or not, a guardian angel was a he. So that was settled. He sighed contentedly and gazed at the tree tops opposite, and would have been awed but not unduly surprised to see guardian angels circling above them, flapping their wings in a powerful if cumbersome manner.

None appeared, which was a pity for all of them.

He began to pick at the grass, thinking now about something he had read somewhere to the effect that out in that void through which the earth was hurtling so perilously there were black holes which could suck a man in, flatten him like a piece of thin cardboard, and retain him there forever. He could name several people he wouldn't mind seeing sucked into a black hole.

It was September, but they had taken a chance on the weather for the picnic, and the gamble paid off. It was an exceptionally warm day for the time of year – hot, even – and the trees and shrubs in the Oxfordshire country-side were making the most of it and getting a move on before the winter arrived.

Harry King noted the red haze of some hedge fuchsias without emotion, because at that time red was a colour like any other. It had no sinister associations for him. Admittedly, blood was always red. He had read autopsy reports on one or two dead aristocrats but seen no indication of blue blood; or come to that, of yellow bellies or white livers.

So blood was red. So what? So nothing, on the day of the picnic – or picnics, rather, because there had been two. Madge Owen had brought the lunch. They had used Owen's Triumph Toledo, and shared the cost of the petrol and everything else without argument or embarrassment, like the old friends they were.

The sun was still warm at a quarter to four when they turned off the main Chipping Norton–Burford road into a narrow lane bordered by mixed woods, and pulled up on a flat patch of grass in the shade of a big beech tree. But there was a change in the atmosphere. The air had almost the same damp heat as at lunchtime, but there was now a stillness, as though the birds, such small animals as might be around and even most of the larger insects were finding the oppressive temperature too much for them. Only certain flies came buzzing out of the wood to inspect the picnic party.

'Glorious!' said Madge, who liked any form of heat, dry or moist.

'Won't last,' said her husband happily.

'That's just like you, Bill Owen,' Madge snapped. 'Typical, putting a damper on things.'

'It's not me that's going to dampen you, dear.' He was swiping ineffectually at a dozen flies slowly circling round his head. 'Bloody flies – storm flies, that's what they are, mark my words, dear.'

They spread two car rugs on the grass in the shade and ate a few of Madge's cucumber sandwiches. Laura and Harry King had drunk some cold limejuice and water out of one of the two Thermos flasks Madge had brought with her. She and Bill drank strong tea from the other. Neither heat nor sultry weather could put them off their afternoon cups of hot sweet tea.

After a while, King got up and stood looking around at the sky. It was blue overhead, and there were no distant clouds, but on the horizon the blue was less bright and was tinged with yellow and grey.

'I think Bill's right,' he said. 'There is going to be a storm.'

Owen looked at his wife triumphantly. 'I said it wouldn't last, dear.' He was still swiping at the flies with a rolled-up newspaper. 'You don't get these flies without a storm being near.'

King laughed. 'It's that muck you put on your hair that attracts them, Bill. You want to try Vaseline.'

Owen began to say Vaseline meant dirty pillow cases, but stopped, head raised, listening. Laura and Madge also raised their heads and all four listened to the noise coming from the wood on the other side of the lane.

It sounded like bodies threshing about in the undergrowth. There were occasional thuds, and what sounded like two raised boyish voices shouting at each other. Sometimes in excitement, sometimes in alarm.

'Sounds like two kids have a scrap,' Harry King said tolerantly.

The crashing in the undergrowth drew near enough for them to make out some of the words now: 'It's over there . . . behind the tree . . . watch out . . . go on, slosh it . . . I'm trying to, aren't I? . . . watch out for its mate, Jim . . . it's gone under the rhododendron bush, Bert . . . you go the other side and get it when I drive it out . . . crikey, it's coming back . . .'

There were more thuds, then silence for a minute or two.

'Not scrapping – killing something,' Laura said in a low voice.

She brushed the light wavy hair back from her forehead, amber eyes fixed intently on the wood – where before there had been noise and excitement, and where now there was only silence.

Then there was noise again, but this time of a more orderly and leisurely kind, as whoever it was pushed through the bushes towards the lane. Some sort of discussion was taking place, and the words 'nest', 'stepladder', 'dangerous', 'young ones', and 'mate' were audible.

Then the undergrowth parted and two boys stepped on to the grass and began to walk quickly along the road towards the picnickers. One looked to be about fourteen years old, the other a year or two younger. They wore old grey shorts and grubby white short-sleeved shirts, and had fair tousled hair and the healthy shining faces of country lads. They could have been brothers.

The taller of the two was carrying something to which he had tied a piece of string, and as he walked he swung in backwards and forwards at his side.

King called out: 'What you got there, son?'

The boys came off the road and went up to the picnickers.

'Snake, big 'un,' said the tall boy.

'Bert killed it,' said the other boy, admiringly. 'We chased it and Bert sloshed it with his ash stick.'

'Jim was climbing in a tree, see, and he saw this nest of snakes in a hole in the tree,' Bert said. 'Dozens of 'em. All squirming an' sliding and slipping, and a big 'un, too, an' it reared up at Jim, waving its head from side to side and hissing. Would 'ave attacked him.'

'Not *this* one,' explained Jim, holding up the dead snake. 'Bert saw *this* one at the foot of the tree. It's a mate of the one in the nest. It was jolly hard to kill. It made off and wriggled and lashed around, but Bert got it on the head in the end.'

'We're going to get our dad to come with his gun,' said Bert. 'He'll kill the other one.'

'Bang!' explained the younger boy called Jim. 'Blow its head off, see!'

'An' we'll bring a stepladder,' Bert said. 'An' when he's shot the other big 'un we'll go up and rake the little 'uns out and kill 'em when they fall to the ground.'

Laura King was staring with horror at the excited lads, her eyes wide and unblinking. Her usually tawny complexion had a red patch on each cheekbone.

'Why?' she asked explosively.

'Why what, missus?' Bert asked.

'Why kill them?' she said in a voice now hardly above a whisper. 'Why? Why?'

The boys looked at her in astonishment.

'Snakes is dangerous,' Bert muttered.

'You got to kill them,' Jim said. 'They bite you an' you die. Everybody knows that,' he added pityingly.

Owen had stopped trying to swat flies and was glaring at the dead snake held by Bert, and at Laura. King thought he had turned pale, and was surprised. Owen said:

'The lad's right. It's no good waiting till you're bitten, Laura.'

She took no notice of him. She looked at the astonished boys, her eyes still blazing.

'Didn't they tell you at school the difference between poisonous adders, with a zig-zag pattern on their backs, and harmless grass snakes?'

'You gotter kill it before you can look at it proper, 'aven't you?' said the boy Jim obstinately.

'Course you 'ave,' agreed the boy Bert. 'Stands to reason, an' anyway they're slimy, slippery, rotten things.'

Laura King, standing upright, feet apart, hands on hips, turned her strange coloured searchlight eyes on him.

13

'Show me the one you're holding.'

The boy swung his right arm back and tossed the dead snake towards her, a sullen expression on his face. It fell at her feet with a leaden thud.

Owen, who had been sitting on the ground beside her, gasped and rolled away sideways, staring round-eyed at the snake. He was panic-stricken and white in the face, and scrambled to his feet.

'Take that thing away!' he said loudly. 'Go on, take it away!'

King, who had lit a pipe to keep the flies off, took it from his mouth and said indulgently: 'It's dead, Bill. Not to worry.'

Laura stepped forward, picked up the dead reptile and looked accusingly at the boys. 'See! Grass snake!'

She ran one hand along its body. 'And snakes aren't slimy or slippery. They all have dry, firm skins. And they do some good, eating insects and things, and they're more afraid of people than people are of them – *usually*,' she added, softly, and looking towards Bill Owen.

She handed the dead snake back to the older boy. 'So you're not going to kill the others, are you?'

'No, missus,' they both replied together, and set off down the road, glancing over their shoulders towards the wood as though to pinpoint a position.

She didn't think the young snakes had much future, whatever had been said. She sat down again, and Bill Owen dropped to the ground and sat beside her as before. Reluctantly, it seemed to Harry.

Nobody spoke for a little while. They were still embarrassed by Owen's lack of self-control. As if to break the tension, Laura said: 'Poor old Bill, I didn't know you felt that way about snakes. I quite admire them. Beautifully marked and slim, good looking, and more intelligent than people think. Like rats. I admire rats, too. Cheer up, Bill, it's all over,' she said and put out her right hand to pat him on the shoulder. But he shrank away quickly, as if even the touch of a hand which had itself touched a snake was abhorrent to him.

Harry King turned his big straight nose towards his wife, and tried to rectify the situation. 'We're all afraid of something. I've been driven out of bed by a big, harmless moth, as you know, Laura.'

'Yes, I do know.'

'Laura's afraid of spiders. What are you afraid of, Madge?'

'Death. I don't want to snuff it,' she said in her usual brisk, firm voice. 'Otherwise nothing that I can think of. Oh, and complete darkness, like when a train goes through a tunnel and the carriage lights don't work. But I don't panic, do I, Bill?'

'No, Madge doesn't panic,' agreed Owen.

'Everybody can control themselves, if they've got to,' Laura King said, and realised it was a tactless remark.

'I hadn't *got to*, had I?' Owen said, and Laura made it worse, by murmuring, 'No, but I don't know what those kids thought. You're a big boy now, Bill. Good job they didn't know you're supposed to be a tough cop.'

Harry King was appalled. It was all out of character. Laura was usually gentle and tactful.

'Who cares what the kids thought?' asked Madge sharply. 'My Bill's not afraid of anything that *matters*, are you, Bill?'

Owen's big lips parted in a grateful smile. Madge was picking about round the edge of the rug, separating beechnut husks from pine needles, building up a little pyramid of husks. Laura King said:

'If you saw them at close hand, Bill, saw *me* pick up one or two, you might – '

'One or two what?' asked Owen, as if he didn't understand what she meant, or couldn't believe his ears.

'Baby snakes.'

'You must be out of your tiny mind; I wouldn't go near the bloody things.'

'You would if you had to.'

'He doesn't have to, does he?' Madge said loudly.

'No, he doesn't *have* to,' Laura King admitted reluctantly. 'But I made Harry catch a moth in his bare hands, and after that he didn't mind them any more, did you, Harry?'

'Not much. A little bit, but not much.'

'You wouldn't panic in front of a couple of kids if a moth settled on your arm, would you?' asked Laura.

She seemed obsessed. Harry King couldn't understand it. He turned his wife's question, and said:

'Perhaps I was never actually *afraid* of moths – they just bring back nasty memories. When I was a kid I used to read by a candle which stood on the bedside table. Moths would fly in and flutter round the naked flame, and I knew what was going to happen, and used to wait for the sizzle, and sometimes they were only half burnt and flopped on to the bedside table, fluttering. It was horrid, and – '

Laura laughed. 'I'm not going to fry the snakes, Bill, they won't sizzle. From what the boys said, and the way they glanced back, they're in a hole in that oak. Come on, Bill, I bet I can cure you.'

Owen shivered and shook his head.

'Oh, come on, have a go,' wheedled Laura King.

'Let him be,' Madge said irritably.

'I'm only trying to help him for the future,' Laura said.

'Well, he doesn't need your help.'

'Okay, okay – steady on,' said Harry King quickly.

'Take it easy, you two,' agreed Bill Owen. 'Don't want to spoil a nice day spatting, Madge. Laura didn't mean anything.'

The conversation petered out. Nobody said anything for a while. Then, speaking almost to herself, Laura said: 'They're only *little* snakes, and they won't bite.' She shuffled forward on the rug and began to collect the remains of the picnic. While she did so, Madge took a used paper napkin, tidily put a couple of cigarette butts in it, added some more rubbish and the pyramid of beechnut husks, lightly screwed up the paper, handed it to Laura and said:

'A present for you, dear. Let bygones be bygones, etc.'

Laura King took it and reached forward to add it to the other rubbish in the picnic bag, dropped it, and screamed as the two small spiders ran out of it and on the back of her hand. She rolled over backwards and sideways, as Owen had done, frantically shook her hand till the spiders dropped to the ground, and then leaped to her feet and moved a couple of yards from the rug.

'They're only *little* spiders,' Madge said, 'and they won't bite, dear.'

Laura King was white and trembling. 'Don't ever do anything like that again, Madge!' she said. 'Not ever, ever, or I'll kill you.'

'I was only trying to help for the future, dear,' Madge said, and smiled, 'and *I'll* kill *you* if you go on at Bill about snakes.'

Harry King had risen to his feet again, and was looking at a horizon which was darkening ominously. The storm flies were more active than ever. 'We'd better go,' he said sadly.

He did not think things would ever be the same again between them. Between Bill Owen and himself, yes — but as a foursome, no. The rain storm would pass. The other storm wouldn't, not entirely. It was a pity.

Owen was quiet on the way home, though in the back of the car the two wives seemed to have resumed a friendly relationship, at least on the surface, and were grumbling about the price of goods in the shops. King thought the only good thing about inflation was that it provided a common ground on which people could agree.

But Owen remained silent. As they approached London, King said: 'What's up, Bill? Not still thinking about snakes?'

'One snake. And not a dead one.'

'Has it got a record?'

'It has; five volumes. Remember what happened at the Old Bailey, Harry?'

'I do.'

King remembered, all right. It was the last time he had seen Buller.

Buller in the dock, found guilty of possessing and

dealing in heroin and other drugs, interrupting the judge as sentence was passed. Buller screaming threats and obscenities until he was hustled, struggling, downstairs to the cells. Buller shouting: 'I'll get you, copper! I bloody will, an' I'll get you where it'll hurt most, copper! And then I'll go on getting you, and I'll get you personally in the end, copper!'

King had just smiled. He was used to threats from crooks and gangsters. They rarely tried to carry them out. And Buller, with the tall massive build, the heavy white face, the big teeth, the thick nose and fierce black eyes – could Buller be different? He didn't think so.

'Been out on parole for over three months now,' said Owen disgustedly. 'Got three years; did one – then out on parole. Makes you sick. Why do we bother? You want to watch it, Harry.'

'The buzz is that he's gone legitimate, Bill.'

'If you believe that you'll believe anything. How legitimate?'

'Gone into business. Don't know the details yet.'

Owen made a noise which was between a grunt and a snort, but for a long time said nothing. He was immersed in his own thoughts and his own attempts to recall the reason for a worry which lurked in his mind. If he could identify it and find the cause he felt that he could cope with it. But he couldn't. He didn't even know if it was something he had seen or something he had dreamed about in a nightmare. Or if it came to his mind via another route altogether: a route he travelled once in a while alone.

He only knew that it had something to do with snakes. Not the dead snake; possibly the baby snakes. And it had been the cause of his violent reaction at the picnic.

That was all he knew. That, and the fact that it was totally evil.

CHAPTER TWO

Superintendent Harry King retired from the Met earlier than anybody expected – quite suddenly, soon after the picnic, and before the chestnut trees had scattered the ground with their fruit.

He retired some years before he had to. There was nothing unusual about that. Many officers do so in order to draw a pension and still be young enough to start in a new line of business. Some become security advisers, mostly to do with theft and burglary prevention, in big firms. A few start up detective agencies of their own, dealing with domestic troubles involving unfaithful husbands or wives, or assisting insurance companies in cases of suspected fraud.

When asked point-blank why he had done it, his reply was as colourless as his appearance. He would remove his pipe from his mouth, shrug, and say: 'Oh, I don't know. For one reason and another.'

There were two main reasons. One was a dispute with an Assistant Commissioner, during a discussion about long-term plans, when King had faithfully pressed Bill Owen's qualifications for promotion. His arguments had been turned down, or if not turned down completely at least accorded no more than a nod and a tacit acknowledgement that they had been noted. The implication was that they had not been accepted. No reason was given. It was a serious reflection on King's judgement. For years he had given Bill Owen good annual reports, stressing his intelligence, dedication, and hard work; omitting any reference to Owen's tendency to yield to Celtic 'hunches' and go off on often useless and exhausting trails. But the clear implication now was that the good reports were not justified.

Why?

After the distressing conference on long-term planning Harry King returned to his room at the Yard in a bad mood. It was composed partly of distress at the thought of Bill Owen's coming disappointment, and partly of annoyance that his judgement had been criticised. He was in a distinct huff. It was still a long way, in emotional distance, from the anger which developed later, but it was only a short way in time.

He was about to pass Bill Owen's room on the way to his own, but suddenly changed his mind, flung open Owen's door and slammed it behind him.

'What's up with you?' Owen asked.

King leaned against the door, and paused to choose his words. The contrast between the two men was even more marked within the confines of the austere room. King, thin-lipped, colourless, grey; Owen florid, with full red lips, dark hair, with large brown eyes like big moist marbles.

King thought Owen might as well have it now, straight from the shoulder.

'I've been having a jaw with the top brass. About the future. I'm going as soon as I can. They don't know it yet, but I am, very soon. And, Bill – I don't think you're going to take over my job. It wasn't what they said, it was what they didn't say. They don't trust my judgement. I did my best for you. It's a slap in the face for me, too. I'm sorry. I did my best for you,' he repeated.

Chief Inspector Owen's eyes flickered a couple of times. He licked his thick lips.

'I'm sure you did your best,' he said after a pause. 'It's the way the cookie crumbles, Harry. Madge'll take it hard, but –'

'Yes, Madge will take it badly. So will Laura.'

'I didn't know Laura cared,' said Owen with an odd expression on his face.

At that, King turned and slipped out of the room like an embittered grey ghost.

When he got back to his office he found a typewritten letter on his desk. It was from Mrs Mary Plummer, of the Sure Friendship Bureau, and, in keeping with her character, was brief and to the point:

Dear Mr King,
We met during the investigation connected with the Sidney Shaw case.* I would like to have a word with you. Perhaps you would kindly ring me.
Yours sincerely,
Mary Plummer.

He supposed she wished to fill in some detail about the case which she had suddenly recalled, and thought of passing it over to one of the officers who had been

* See *The Marriage Bureau Murders* by John Bingham (Macmillan)

23

mainly involved. But, instead, he reached for the telephone, and dialled the number of the office, near the Thames Embankment which, from the letter, she apparently still used despite its awful associations with Shaw.

From the little he had seen of her, he had formed a good impression of the woman. She answered the phone herself. After the usual courtesies, inquiries about each other's health, about which neither of them probably cared much, he glanced at his wristwatch. He had been with the top brass about an hour, and with Bill Owen for ten minutes. It was ten-thirty now.

'Do you want to call here, Mrs Plummer?'

'I'm alone in the office.'

'I'll call on you. After lunch. About 2.30.'

'Fine. I'll have coffee ready.'

'No need to bother. Can you give me some idea—?'

'Not on the phone,' she interrupted. 'See you, Mr King.'

He replaced the receiver.

Consideration of anything she had to say would help to quieten the resentment which still swirled around inside him. But he spent the morning brooding sullenly over his talk with the Assistant Commissioner. Once or twice he tried to read some reports, but they meant nothing to him, his mind being too occupied with Owen, and Madge Owen, and his own pride.

After a canteen lunch he decided that a brisk walk to her office would provide additional therapy. In the event, he arrived ten minutes early; but when she answered the bell she seemed glad to see him. She led him into her office, and asked him to sit down in an easy chair; not opposite the desk where she herself sat,

24

but placed at an angle so that a possibly embarrassed client would not need to sit eyeball-to-eyeball with her.

Mary ('Plummy') Plummer, once junior partner in the Sure Friendship Bureau, was not the sort of woman to allow the misfortune which befell Sidney Shaw, the senior partner, to ruin what had been developing into a nice business, an interesting and lucrative occupation for her middle age. Although admittedly, That Nasty Affair (as she called it), and the subsequent revelation of the nature of Sidney Shaw's character had shocked her, even made her feel queasy for a few moments as the truth broke through the soothing bromides and platitudes of the police.

A tough job lay ahead now, she knew that, and was determined to tackle it.

She made a curiously birdlike impression. She was small and dressed in black and white – a black skirt and a frilly white blouse, magpie colours. Slim legs and arms. Ordinary body, medium height, neither fat nor thin. Black hair, probably dyed. Round face, made up, and a thin nose. Brown eyes. Large tortoise-shell coloured framed spectacles tilted upwards at the sides, to give a faintly demon-like look. These she took off and replaced frequently. The basic birdlike impression was enhanced by a habit she had of cocking her head on one side from time to time, especially when she was awaiting the answer to a question. Recalling his impression of her in the past, such as it was, he thought she had been more motherly then. She seemed to have sharpened up since.

Age? Perhaps late forties, perhaps early fifties. Nowadays you couldn't tell.

'I've got a problem,' she said, abruptly putting an end to chit-chat about the weather.

Superintendent King gave a wintry smile.

She began to open drawers in her desk. She found the file she wanted, pulled it out and began to flick through it. Meanwhile King was gazing round the room. He noted the long golden curtains and grey carpet, some reproductions of Old Masters on the walls, a large house-plant on a small table by the window, and a couple of figurines on the mantelpiece above the fire.

Apart from that it was sparsely furnished, containing only her own big mahogany desk, which she had moved from Sidney Shaw's room next door, two fairly comfortable easy chairs, and a third, smaller chair. The office gave a general impression of a disciplined comfort, like the headmistress's room in a reform school for delinquent girls. She had often decided to make it more homely, for the sake of shy and nervous prospective clients, but had not yet got around to it.

Eventually, she slapped the file shut and handed it to King.

'Read that. It won't take long.'

The file contained half a dozen letters. King took it reluctantly. The letters were all from new clients. One read:

Dear Madam,

I was under the impression that my association with your bureau was a confidential one. Unfortunately this does not prove to be the case.

I am, as you are aware, an insurance broker, and have been extremely embarrassed recently by badinage from colleagues in the same line of business. 'Well, got spliced yet?' and 'When's the wedding, what's she like?' are typical of the type of remarks which have recently greeted me in City lunchtime taverns, and even in my golf club.

From investigations which I undertook, it appears likely that some member of your firm telephoned my office one morning giving the name of your bureau and asking to speak to me. The message, as it happens, did not reach me, since I was confined to my bed with a bad attack of jaundice at the time, and it had been mislaid by the time I returned.

I do not wish to have further association with you, shall not, of course, be renewing my annual subscription, and, as you have been, as I see it, in breach of contract with me, I shall be glad if you will return the amount of my down payment by return of post.

Yours faithfully,
 Philip Goodman.

'Did you?'

'Did I what?' asked Mary Plummer.

'Return his money.'

'You must be joking.'

The second letter was more curt and made its point in a couple of paragraphs:

Dear Madam,

I have been informed by an unimpeachable source, which I do not propose to reveal – he is the head of

27

*a well-known firm of private detectives – that your
so-called bureau is in effect nothing more than a
call-girl agency. I am seeking a respectable wife.*

*I do not need the services of an organisation like
yours to fix for me what might be termed in theatrical
jargon a one night stand, and am therefore cancelling
my subscription.*

   Yours etc.
      L. R. Brown.

There were three other letters, two from women, all
containing complaints of one sort or another. They had
arrived at intervals of about a fortnight, and Mary
Plummer at first had taken no special notice, regarding
it all as the luck of the game.

But one had given her real cause for thought. It
ended:

   *I am still in hospital, where I have said I was the
   victim of a mugging by a thug. I hope to be out
   tomorrow, slightly scarred, but otherwise undamaged.
   I think it was a man in woman's clothes.*

Mulling over the complaints file and re-reading the
letters, she had noted, she said, that most of the complaints implied a breach of confidence. This was absurd.
Her only regular assistant was Alice Caldwell, married,
with one child, whose husband was an ill-paid minor
local government official. Like Mary Plummer, she
needed the money she earned, and the money depended
on the business.

Mary Plummer said she regarded the letters campaign

as Phase Two in what she called the Marriage Bureau War.

Superintendent King raised his eyebrows enquiringly. 'And Phase One?'

'Weeks ago.'

'Tell me,' he said patiently, though his mind was still preoccupied with Bill Owen's bad luck.

On St Valentine's Day, Mary Plummer had let herself into the bureau office, a suite of four rooms on the ground floor of Bellecourt, a modern six-storey building. She didn't expect to find a Valentine, she said, but on the other hand she was horrified by what she did find.

It was a Monday morning, about nine o'clock, and the office was cold because the heating had been off all weekend. She went into her own room, pulled the curtains widely apart, put down her handbag, hung up her coat and scarf, warmed her hands for a few moments in front of the electric fire, and then went next door to switch on the fire in the general office where the files were kept in their steel cabinets and where Alice Caldwell worked.

Alice was due in at ten o'clock but she was always late, Mary Plummer thought, and opened the door of the general office; she stopped on the threshold, shocked and bewildered, and felt the tears welling up in her eyes.

The filing cabinets had been broken into; files and cards were scattered about the floor. The side of Alice Caldwell's desk showed burns where cigarettes had been stubbed out, and the stubs littered the carpet.

Mary 'Plummy' Plummer stared at it all, motionless

except for the movement of her shoulders as she sobbed. Then she made herself a cup of coffee and started to clear up the mess.

When Alice Caldwell arrived, Alice said:

'Some enemy hath done this.'

'Some enemy hath,' agreed Mary Plummer. 'I didn't know I had any.'

'Maybe not enemies – just rivals.'

Mary stared at her.

'You mean *that* lot?'

'Yes – *that* lot. The Round Circle crowd.'

'But why? Why didn't they just burn or steal the cards and files? They haven't even stolen the petty cash. Why?'

'Your guess is as good as mine,' Alice Caldwell said, tight-lipped and pale. 'But I would think – to judge by the number of cigarette ends – that there were at least two of them and they spent the time photographing names and addresses and confidential parts of our files.'

It was then Mary Plummer had thought of writing to the only police officer she had ever really known, because this was no ordinary job and the future might not be ordinary, either. But she had procrastinated. Then the letters of complaint began to arrive.

Now she looked at King and said: 'They've been leafleting Earls Court Road and Shepherd's Bush areas – my territory.'

'Did you tell the police about the break-in?'

'What was the use? Nothing was stolen. And the police are so busy.'

Harry King sighed. Now he certainly wished he had

30

handed her letter over to another officer. He felt it was not his day.

It was not, and it was not over yet.

'What do you expect me to do, Mrs Plummer?'

'About the break-in and the letters? Nothing.'

King felt a surge of relief.

Mary Plummer cleared her throat, adjusted her spectacles, tilted her head, birdlike, and said: 'It's all part of a campaign, you know – to close me down or take me over on knock-down terms.' She shook her head. 'No way, no dice, Mr King. I won't let it happen.' Then she went on, 'I've got a different idea. You may think me impertinent, because we don't really know each other. But I wondered whether you might care to join me as a partner. A junior partner,' she added hastily.

King looked at her, startled. Then he thought for a moment. His mind was still filled with resentment against the top brass. But he shook his head.

'No, Mrs Plummer. For one thing, I've no capital.'

'Yes, you have, Mr King. Experience. I need it. I think things are going to get worse before they get better – if they do get better. I need protection and advice. We saw a good deal of each other during the Shaw case, and we got on all right. You're a police officer, and a successful one.'

'That's a matter for debate,' King said bleakly.

'I suppose you'll be thinking of retiring soon? You won't want to do nothing. The way things are going, you'll be fully stretched here. And there's money in it. Think it over.'

He recalled his interview with the Assistant Commissioner. It wouldn't have been so bad if they had given some reason; he might have been able to cope with that. Ironically, their blank silence was the biggest slap in the face he had experienced in all his career. Even now the memory of it brought a flush to his grey, tired face.

But subconsciously he must have been turning over Mary Plummer's problems in his mind, quickly and professionally, for he suddenly nodded, as though agreeing with his thoughts, and said:

'You need to have clients vetted, if you can. Names passed over the C.R.O. files – that's the Criminal Records Office. To see if there's any past history of – '

'Rape. Assault. All that?' Mary Plummer nodded her head vigorously.

'It wouldn't be one-hundred-per-cent security by any means, but it would be a start.'

'It would. If one could arrange it.'

Superintendent Harry King was always at his best when faced with a challenge, a problem which seemed insoluble, and now he said slowly, almost to himself: 'I wonder.' Then, more loudly, he added: 'I know a senior officer. Very dedicated man. As interested in crime *prevention* as crime *detection*. I wonder – '

'Now you're talking,' said Mary Plummer enthusiastically. 'But meanwhile – ' she broke off, opened a side drawer of her desk and took out a tape recorder and cassette.

'After what I call the softening up, Phases 1 and 2 – the break-in, the anonymous letters to clients – I had an offer.'

King listened attentively.

32

'In addition to a few written notes, I use this – hidden in my half-open drawer, of course. It might put clients off if they knew. Chap called Buller rang the other day and asked to see me. I thought it was a possible client, and agreed. I switched on when he arrived. Like to listen?'

'If you wish,' he replied, his heart beating faster.

She leaned towards the recorder and moved a switch. Harry King watched her while the memory bells jangled in his mind. The scene at the Old Bailey; Buller's threats. Buller on parole. Buller allegedly 'going legitimate'. And before that, Buller snarling under interrogation, hate flaring from his smouldering eyes.

Buller, Frederick Buller? Superintendent King frowned. He was too old and grey a fox entirely to discount coincidence.

Nothing of interest came from the tape for some fifteen seconds. Then there was the noise of a door opening and closing, and Mary Plummer and a man speaking:

'Good morning, Mr Buller.'

'Good morning.'

'Sit down. Care for a cup of tea?'

'No, thank you.'

Lengthy chit-chat about the weather.

Silence. Sound of Mary Plummer giving a little cough, clearing her throat, getting off on the wrong foot, saying:

'Well, Mr Buller, I hope we can be of some help. I'll give you one of our forms. Just obvious questions – work, hobbies, likes, dislikes – all that: you can fill it in, in the next room here if you like, or take it home and post it. Then we'll complete the formalities.'

'You got it wrong,' the full-throated male voice came from the cassette. 'I'm not in the market for a wife.'

Harry King stiffened. He was certain now about the voice.

'Oh – I thought you wanted to become – one of our subscribers, Mr Buller.'

'Not really.'

'Sorry.'

'Wanted to talk about something else, really.'

'So sorry, Mr Buller.'

' 'S all right, Mrs Plummer. No harm done, no skin off your nose, as the saying is.'

'So, what – ?'

'Mind if I smoke?'

'Please do. I'm afraid I can't offer you a cigarette. I don't smoke.'

'Got my own, thanks.' Sound of scraping. Probably an ash-tray being pushed in Buller's direction across the top of the desk. 'Want to talk about business, Mrs Plummer,' Buller said.

'What business?'

'This business.'

Mary Plummer coughed. The tape recorder crackled. There was silence for ten seconds.

'What about this business?' she asked at length. Her voice had lost the plummy note she sometimes used with clients.

As he listened, King sat very still. He was recalling his own voice recently telling Bill Owen that Buller was just a big mouth, and saying much the same thing to

34

Laura. He was remembering something else he had said to Owen: 'He won't try anything; I wish he would.' But Owen had shaken his head doubtfully. So had Laura the other day.

There were probably lots of Bullers in the world, but this voice seemed to be the voice of Fred Buller. 'What did he look like, Mrs Plummer?'

'Big, hefty fellow. Dark hair. Pale face, black looking eyes. Odd way of tilting sideways in his chair. Rolling gait when he walked.'

King nodded. The voice, description, and ruthless methods fitted. He felt something odd: he thought he saw a red mist rising from the side of the chair Buller had sat in, where he himself was now sitting. His heart was beating faster again, thudding madly in his chest. Supposing Laura and Owen were right, and Buller were not just a big mouth? Supposing there were red blood in Harry King's house, even now? He had expected the voice on the tape to shout, 'I'll get you, copper, I'll get you where it hurts most!'

And if Buller got Laura, that was where it would hurt most.

'Are you all right, Mr King?'

He found that if he forced himself to breathe deeply and very slowly, the heart stopped thumping, and the red mist around him dispersed.

'Are you all right, Mr King?' she asked again.

The coffee cup and saucer were slanting sideways on his knee. Mary Plummer pushed back her chair and took the cup and saucer from him.

'I'm all right, thank you,' he murmured. 'Sorry!'

'Sure?'

'Sure,' he said, still breathing deeply and slowly, seeing the red mist slowly dispersing, seeing real colours take its place. The brown of the desk, the brown of her puzzled eyes, the grey of the carpet, the gold of the cushions.

'What's the trouble?' she asked softly.

He shrugged, waved a hand.

'Touch of blood pressure?'

'Maybe. I'll ask my croaker,' he replied in a dull, uninterested voice, controlling his breathing again because he had to.

Slowly in. Slowly out. Blood pressure? Blood. Laura's blood. But Laura had to be all right. He shook his head.

'Switch on again, please. I'm quite all right. Just a touch of giddiness. Gone now. Switch on,' he said again, urgently.

He saw Mary Plummer back-track the tape to where she had said:

'What about this business Mr Buller?'

Buller's voice answered.

'Taken a bit of a bashing, hasn't it? No fault of yours, of course.'

'It had a setback, yes. But – '

'Setback? It had a bashing. Like I said. You know it, an' I know it, no good messing about with words.'

There was silence. King could imagine her looking birdlike, intent. Then came her recorded voice, blurred by traffic noise from outside:

'What makes you think that, Mr Buller?'

Rustle and movement noise as Buller shifted in his chair.

'You know it – I know it. Ernie Dicker told me.'

Silence. Then Mary Plummer's voice, puzzled:

'Do I know him?'

'Mr Dicker? Runs the Round Circle Agency with me.'

'Oh, yes? Well, I don't have the pleasure of – '

'If you don't know him, you'll get to know him.'

Short, forced laugh. Mary Plummer speaking tartly:

'I get to know whom I want to know, Mr Buller.'

'That's no way to start a long and beautiful friendship.'

'Who says I want to start one?'

'I do. Mr Dicker, he says so, too. Right? That's why I'm here. Right?'

King wished he wouldn't keep saying 'Right?'

Sound of a tea cup being replaced on a saucer.

'Are you his hatchet man, Mr Buller, if that's the expression? I suppose he sent you here to – '

'Nobody *sends* me nowhere. Ernie Dicker, he started the Round Circle mob, right? Him and me. He put the cash in, I do the organising, you know? We split the dough. It's going to be big, Mrs Plummer. He's got capital. He's branching out, kind of going international, see? Started in London, then we'll spread to the provinces, York, Huddersfield, Southampton – you name it, we'll be there, maybe France and Germany, America. We're going places, Ernie and me. Right? And he's got other interests.'

Mary Plummer's voice, deceptively soft and polite now:

'I'm so glad for you.'

Buller's voice, also now soft and polite:

'That's better, Mrs Plummer, that's much better, nice and friendly. Right? 'Cos Ernie, he says to me yesterday, he says, "Fred, you trot along and see the Sure Friendship lot, have a word with Mrs Plummer." He knows about you, Mrs P., he's got ways of finding out. You know?'

'No, I don't know. But go on.'

' "Make her an offer," he says. "Make Mrs P. an offer, Fred. I got to go back to Liverpool in a couple of weeks. Fix it up before I go, she could do with a helping hand, poor lady. We could use Mrs P. personally." '

'And the offer?'

Mary Plummer switched off the recorder and looked at Harry King.

'I could see what he was beating up to, of course. At that moment he didn't remind me of a shark; I thought of a bird of prey hovering over what it thought was a dying animal – sitting in the branch of a tree, stropping its beak in anticipation of a meal.'

King nodded automatically, only half listening to her, his mind's eye on mist which was going to turn red again.

'Let's have the rest of it,' he said.

She switched on. Buller's voice came into the room again, throaty and persuasive.

' "Make her an offer, fix it up, Fred," Ernie says. "Invite her to join us, and bring all her nice files, of course. We could do with a lady like her – maybe for Newcastle or Huddersfield, or somewhere. She's a tough dolly, I'm told, we could do with her." So what about it, Mrs P., what about it? In principle, just in principle.

38

Right? I reckon we won't quarrel about details. Ernie's big minded, he thinks big, does Ernie. What about it?'

'Thank Mr Dicker, but tell him it's not on. I like to paddle my own canoe.'

Sound of a couple of clicks, like a cigarette lighter being used. Sound of two deep breaths, as of smoke being drawn in, then expelled from the lungs. Then Buller, mocking, threatening:

'Your canoe's sprung a leak, dear. Watch out it doesn't get stove in, dear. Ernie Dicker, he doesn't like being refused, see? Hard nosed is Ernie, when he don't get what he wants. I got your interests at heart saying that, dear. You're a nice doll – we could get on, we could; work well together. Think it over a bit more, dear.'

'Tell Mr Dickson – '

'Dicker. He don't like people getting his name wrong. Touchy. I'm not: people call me Fuller, Puller, Muller even, don't matter to me. Fred, Ted, Ned, don't matter to Fred Buller, not at all, but Ernie Dicker, he's touchy.'

'Well, tell him that I am not interested in a takeover.'

'Pity to have two mobs competing on the same patch.' The voice was despairing, like a messenger who doesn't want to carry bad news back to a barbaric potentate.

'Tell him to choose another patch. My patch is the Earls Court area, Hammersmith, north Kensington, Shepherd's Bush, and – '

There was a long silence, broken only by the sound of a dog barking in the street and the groan of lorries and cars. Then Buller again: 'Know what I think, Mrs Plummer? The idea crosses my mind – '

Mary Plummer interrupted. Clearly she had been

unable to resist a crack at him. 'I don't know what idea has crossed your mind, but it must be a short journey.' She spoke acidly. 'That's not original, but it'll do. Mr Dicker's tactics aren't original, either. And *they* won't do.'

Sound of somebody sighing deeply, sadly. Then Buller's voice, still throaty, but coming over loudly and clearly, and unexpectedly harsh. 'Know what I think?'

'Must you tell me?'

'I think you're bloody daft, dear, as they say in the vernacular.'

She seemed to be thinking for a few long seconds. Then her voice, prim, school-marmish, slow and deliberate, the words chosen with care:

'And I think that you, Mr Buller, taking Mr Dicker with you, can go and jump in the Thames – as they also say in the vernacular.'

Mary Plummer switched off the recorder.

Harry King sat staring intently at her. His normally pallid face was again suffused and pink with shock from listening to the voice of Buller.

'What did he look like?' he murmured.

'I beg your pardon? Look like? I've told you.'

'Tell me again.'

'Big hefty fellow. Dark hair, pale face, black eyes. Odd way of tilting sideways in the chair. Rolling gait when he walked. Why?'

'He's a crook, gangster type.'

'That doesn't surprise me.'

'It's the way he'd operate, Mrs Plummer.'

But he was not thinking of the marriage agency's

troubles. He was again hearing Bill Owen's voice: 'He won't love you one little bit, Harry.' And hearing Laura's diffident voice with its undertone of fear: 'I saw Buller this morning, darling; it gave me quite a turn. I was at the trial, you remember, I know what he looks like. Saw him this morning, walking near this house.'

Mary put the recorder in a deep drawer of her desk. She said:

'They either want to keep me going, and cut in on the takings; or they want to take me over completely; or close me down. I'll have to watch out: I don't know what for, but I'll have to watch out.'

He still wasn't listening properly.

Mary Plummer said: 'I'd thought of him as a vulture. But as he heaved himself out of his chair to go, and did a sort of half-roll sideways towards the door, I saw he wasn't a vulture; with his great height, and big white face, and large teeth I saw that after all he was a white shark, the deadliest of the sharks, and his idea in his fishy mind was to crunch me, swallow me, turn the sea red.

Red, thought King, yes, he would, he'd turn anything red. King was afraid; desperately afraid for Laura.

So Buller was linked up with this man Ernie Dicker, who must have known of the break-in at the Sure Friendship office. He wondered what Dicker's other business interests were.

Harry King took the plunge. He felt calm now, certain that what he was about to do was necessary.

'We haven't discussed terms yet,' said Mary Plummer.

'They'll be all right. I was going to pack it in at the

Yard, anyway, and I've got a fairly good pension. When do I start? Tomorrow?'

She looked astonished. 'You'll have to give notice – '

'A month, I suppose. I've got a month's leave due to me. I'll take it from tomorrow. I'll give a month's notice when I write my letter of resignation – this afternoon, at the Yard – and go on a month's leave. And not go back. The top brass can sort things out as best they can,' he added bitterly.

Mary Plummer looked surprised but radiant with pleasure. 'That's a great relief to me!'

Buller was the cause of his decision. He knew that. Although he had always referred to Buller with contempt, the sound of the man's voice, and Mary's description of him, had aroused the latent fear of him which had been lurking unacknowledged in his subconscious. Instinctively he felt that anything which brought him into contact with Buller, either directly or indirectly, must pay off somehow. He would get Buller, and get him sent down for a long stretch, a really long stretch next time, and no mistake. How, he didn't know; but he would.

So long as Buller was loose he was a menace. Mary Plummer was right. She needed protection. So did Laura.

Harry King got to his feet.

'Well, that's that. I'll clock in tomorrow.'

'And we'll discuss terms?'

He nodded indifferently. 'We'll hack something out. Can I use your phone?' The fear for Laura was seeping back. He knew he had to take a grip on himself. But he wanted to hear her voice.

'You can use Sidney's old phone. I'll show you.' She led King into the room next to hers. 'There you are. Sidney's room. It's yours now.' She went out, only half closing the door behind her.

Harry King sat down at the empty desk. Before using the phone, he wiped it with his pocket handkerchief, almost automatically, feeling it might still be contaminated by the Sidney Shaw evil. Then he dialled Laura's number and heard her voice; he felt a surge of relief, and said:

'Hello, Lauralie, darling, how are things? You all right?'

'Yes, I'm all right. On the whole. Why shouldn't I be?'

'No reason.'

'There is one thing, though.'

King waited, tense.

'I think I saw Buller again this morning, in this road, passing the house, walking with that rolling gait he has. He paused and looked at the house, and then went on.'

'Sure it was him?'

'Pretty sure. I might have been wrong, of course. But it did make me feel a bit creepy.'

Now it was the old dilemma. Whether to warn her to be very careful, and so scare her, or play it cool. He decided to play it cool.

'I've got some news for you about Buller.'

'What?'

'He's up to some tricks again. Not old tricks, new tricks.'

She did not say anything for a few seconds.

'That doesn't surprise you, does it, Harry?'

'Not really. But I'll get him. I'll fix him for something, good and proper.'

'Be careful, darling.'

'Meaning?'

'He's got a good lawyer. And he's dangerous.'

'He's a menace. He ought to be put away – for the good of the tribe.'

'Be careful, darling,' she said again.

'I've got some other news. Bill won't get my job when I leave.'

There was silence for a moment, then she said: 'That's bad. Madge will be furious.'

'It is – and she will. But I've got some other news.'

'What?'

'Won't tell you on the phone.'

'Good news?'

'I think you'll like it. I hope so, Lauralie love. It'll mean less night work; more evenings together. Fewer evenings on your own.'

He heard her laugh delightedly.

'Oh, good! When does it start?'

'As from tomorrow.'

He heard her sigh, and knew it was a sigh of relief.

'As from tomorrow?'

'That's right. Bye-bye, Lauralie darling.'

'Bye-bye, love. Be seeing you.'

Then he suddenly remembered that he had not told her he would not be home early as promised. He wanted to start clearing up his papers at the office. He shouted quickly into the mouthpiece. 'Lauralie!'

But she had hung up. He thought of ringing back, but shrugged and decided not to do so. She would understand. She was accustomed to disappointingly late home-comings.

Mary Plummer was coming out of her room when he went into the entrance hall, and there was another woman there, a youngish woman in her late twenties or early thirties, who had just let herself into the office with her own key. Harry King automatically registered her appearance: medium height, slim build and legs. Fair hair. Blue eyes. Very delicate, fresh complexion. He heard Mary Plummer greet her.

'Hello, Alice, what – ?'

'Sorry. I couldn't get in earlier this morning, Mary. Had to take Lucy to the doctor. On her birthday too! Been coughing all night. Nothing to worry about, though; I'll just have to keep her in the warm for a day or two. Auntie's looking after her, of course. I've told the Pimlico Kindergarten.'

Mary Plummer nodded. 'It's all right, Alice. Alice, this is Mr Harry King – you remember I wrote to him; he's joining us. Tomorrow.'

'Tomorrow?'

'Tomorrow. Mr King, this is Alice Caldwell – my right hand and arm.'

Alice Caldwell looked at King coolly, appraisingly. 'Glad to meet you. Hope you'll be happy with us.'

'Thank you; I'm sure I will. And now I must be off. I've got a letter to write.'

He smiled briefly at Mary Plummer. But he wasn't thinking of Mary Plummer. He was trying to place Alice Caldwell, to filter out her face and figure from the vast number of people he had met. He had no success. Alice Caldwell, for her part, showed no more interest in him after her first speculative glance, and began taking off her gloves and coat.

Superintendent King, as he still was, tried all the way back to the Yard to place her. Was she somebody he had met professionally? Somebody he had had convicted or interrogated? One of the numerous suspects he had taken an interest in? Unlikely. He would have remembered at least something. Had they had some social meeting in the past? In East Sheen, where he lived? At the club there? Possibly. He would ask Laura that evening. Wives remember other women better than men, especially the good-looking ones whom their husbands have met. And Alice was certainly good-looking.

CHAPTER THREE

While Superintendent King went to the meeting with Mary Plummer which was to alter his life, Chief Inspector Bill Owen sat for some time swallowing his disappointment as best he could. He had managed to put on a stoical front when King had broken the news; but he could not repress a feeling of bitterness.

His emotion did not embrace any feeling of animosity against Harry King. He knew that grey man better than most, certainly better than Madge. Proof that Harry had done his best, if proof were needed, lay in the fact that the Superintendent was soon going to resign.

He wished Harry had not taken the decision. They had worked well together, with never a cross word between them. Who would take his place? Maybe somebody from the uniformed branch or one of the traffic control people, he thought sourly; somebody who would have to learn the tricks of the anti-narcotics circus from square one. He put a stop to that line of thought because it was unfair, and would probably prove to be untrue.

Nevertheless, Bill Owen did not think he would stay on long when Harry left the Yard. He had been thrown to the wolves.

Yet he would be sorry to go. The romantic Welsh side of him was secretly proud of what Harry would call his 'service to the tribe'. Madge, in her outspoken north-country way, always said he had 'too much bloody dedication'. He thought the words too high falutin', and preferred Harry's more down to earth expression.

He sat staring at a big coloured picture, poster size, hanging on the wall opposite him. It showed a side view of a nude girl, curled up inside a big landing net which was being used to scoop her out of the water, like a fish. It had been put there by some joker for a leaving party for one of the secretaries; it was pleasant and original, and not in the least pornographic. But he doubted if the Commissioner would have approved.

The disappointment of Harry's announcement was bad enough, but even more he dreaded breaking the news to Madge. She would blame Laura, that was certain. And she would go on and on. She was a good lass, but he did wish she wouldn't go on and on. What's more, he himself didn't blame Harry or Laura at all. It was sad. The four of them had been happy before the picnic. Since the picnic, mutual invitations had somehow fizzled out.

He unlocked a drawer of his desk, and took out a small cardboard box. It contained smooth round little tablets. He had found a number of them during a drugs raid. He took one out, and decided he would swallow it that evening. Stay out till late. Then he replaced the box in the left-hand top drawer of his desk, and locked the drawer.

When he had done so, his hand remained on the key for a few seconds. He thought he knew the real reason for his being passed over. The A.10 blokes are interested among other things in correct conduct and investigations into complaints. It was not impossible that they had duplicate sets of keys and made periodic clandestine inspections of desk drawers. And the tablets contained LSD.

He knew it was a gamble each time he took one. He rarely did; but when life seemed unbearably humdrum he took the chance. He had done so the night before. And if it went well, the result was unimaginably wonderful. He was one of the lords of the universe, capable of everything, able to meet on level terms anybody who came out of his subconscious, or out of that 'parallel existence' about which Madge was so snooty whenever he said he believed in it. He had met some very interesting characters, often ancient Romans or Greeks. More often Greeks. All colours and all beauty of vision and sound were enhanced; parks and gardens were suddenly filled with fragrant flowers and soft music.

If things went wrong, of course, if he had a bad trip, it was horrifying.

Or at least, it was like that with the old acid. Was it the same now? He wondered, because these new LSD tablets were different. Carter, in the lab., had given them a name of his own. He called them LSD Formula 3. They contained acid, as before, but with a new additive. This caused a form of forgetfulness which cancelled out both good and bad. There was no distinct wonderful memory, but equally there was no detailed memory of horror. All Owen knew was that if you took acid Formula 3 and things went well, you woke up in the morning feeling fit to conquer the world; if you had a bad trip you woke up feeling awful. You forgot the details, even the subject, good or bad. Just as you might forget what you had had for dinner the night before.

But he supposed the additive varied sometimes, in strength and effectiveness, because there had been one or two occasions when he had felt a quickening of the pulses, an excitement – a sensation that he was on the verge of a breakthrough, that for once he would remember the area he had covered on his trip. Not that he would necessarily welcome it; he guessed that. He knew it might be as though he were looking at a corpse in a deep reeking pit seething with venomous snakes.

He had almost had a breakthrough on the day of the picnic. But not quite.

He glanced down again at the drawer in his desk where the acid lay locked away, and again thought about A.10. He shrugged. All he knew was that at least the tablets were probably safer there than at home, where Madge was certain to find them one day, ask questions, take other steps. Women will find anything, anywhere, he thought; not necessarily because they deliberately search, though he wouldn't put that past iron-willed Madge, but because they come across things accidentally, as when they go through pockets before taking suits to the dry cleaners.

He shook his head. He unlocked and opened the drawer again, and took out another small box, a square one containing blue tablets, remains of another narcotic squad raid. Purple Hearts, they had once been known as to the general public, and he'd often wondered why. They were round, not heart-shaped. Admittedly the original ones had been heart-shaped, but never purple. Always blue, pale blue. Sometimes called 'blueies'. Perhaps there was some connection with the American

decoration for courage, the Purple Heart. These drinamyl tablets certainly raised the spirits if you were down
in the dumps.

He would still take the acid in the evening, he re-
flected. Meanwhile he would take a Purple Heart – two,
in fact – to give him courage over the next few hours,
during which time he would have to face Madge and
listen to the waves of indignation which he knew would
pour from her. He swallowed a couple and relocked the
desk drawer.

After half an hour, possibly as a result of the drinamyl,
he suddenly decided to break the news to Madge, by
phone. He listened, sick at heart, to the inevitable explosion. As he had feared, she blamed Harry and Laura
King, especially Laura. Despairingly, he said:

'Look, Madge, take it easy. It's not the end of the
world.'

'I'm going to give her a piece of my mind, Bill Owen,
whatever you say!'

'Calm down, dear. Certainly Harry –'

She interrupted him, voice shaking with that quick
temper he knew so well. 'I'm going to see her at tea time
this afternoon. And after that I'll never speak to her
again!'

'Madge, please!' he began, but he was speaking to
nobody, and he wondered if the heavy bang with which
she had replaced the telephone receiver had damaged the
instrument.

He was settling down to read some reports when the
door opened quietly, and Harry King slid softly into the
room and closed the door behind him. He looked calm

and composed, and sat down in the one easy chair without bothering to take off his overcoat.

'I'm going on a month's leave, Bill, as from tomorrow.'

'Good for you.'

'And I'm not coming back. Well, maybe once, for an hour or two, just finally to clear my desk. Otherwise – no. I'm finished here.'

Harry King spoke quickly, before Bill Owen could protest about the unfairness of leaving his job without time for a proper handover to his successor – whoever that might be.

King described his visit to the Sure Friendship Bureau, and his talk with Mary Plummer. 'It was him all right, Bill. It was Buller.'

'Perhaps it's all part of "going legitimate",' said Owen ironically.

'There's certainly a leak from the agency of some kind, Bill.'

'Alice Caldwell? The girl you saw there?'

'How do I know? Mary swears it can't be, but – ' Harry King frowned. 'I'm going to get Buller – somehow. He's a menace, not fit to be loose.'

'Get him? Why?'

'Laura. She's not safe. You heard what he said when he was sent down.'

'Get him? How?'

'How do I know – yet? But I will.'

'Be careful. He's dangerous,' Owen said, 'and he's got a good lawyer.'

Harry King nodded. 'I know that. Laura knows; she

said the same. She knows, I know. But he's got to be put away – permanently.'

'Six foot underground. Or in a river, Harry; that's the only permanent way – but –'

'I know that, too.'

There was a long silence.

Then Owen shook his head. 'It's not worth the risk of a so-called life sentence, Harry. And meanwhile you're going, leaving me to clear up the mess here. Just like that. In a flash. Thanks a lot.'

'It's my only possible protest to the top brass.'

'Things won't be the same without you,' Bill Owen said, and licked his full red lips. His eyes were wide open and sad. 'I don't expect we'll be seeing much of you. Pity our get-togethers packed up.'

'Women are odd,' said King carefully.

'Laura isn't, but Madge is inclined to get a "thing" about people,' said Owen.

Harry King made no comment. Instead he said:

'We could meet for a beer now and again. Perhaps at a pub in Richmond. Not at the club. Too open.'

'Meaning because of Madge?' Owen looked puzzled.

'Not meaning that. Meaning you could help me – confidentially.'

Owen's puzzled look deepened.

'How? Doing what? Spell it out. Fill me in.'

Harry King explained his plan to help protect the Sure Friendship Agency by having its clients' names passed over the Yard's criminal records files.

Bill Owen shook his head. 'Too risky. Passing confidential information – to an ordinary member of the

53

public, which is what you'll be. I got a pension to think about.'

'You can trust me, Bill. You know that.'

'I know I can trust you, but – '

'Look. I pass you a list of names, each with a number beside it. Okay? Later you pass me a list of numbers – not names,' he went on eagerly, 'just the corresponding numbers; and you just put beside each number the result of the look-up. Maybe O.K., or N.R. "Not recommended". You don't need even to give details, if you don't want to. That's crime prevention. You and I have always agreed that crime prevention is as important as crime detection, haven't we?'

It was a crafty ploy – Owen saw it as such – because it was true. They had often discussed ways and means of improving crime prevention. He said nothing, and King knew he was weakening.

'It's not foolproof,' Owen said at last, uncertainly. But the drinamyl was having its effect. His depression was lifting, being replaced by a feeling of confidence. Temporary, he knew, but better than nothing. And if he left the office soon, he would be able to cope with Madge's inevitable tantrum.

'Not foolproof,' King agreed, 'but better than nothing. Anyway, you might save a girl's life – or a man's reputation. I wouldn't put it past the Round Circle crowd to infiltrate my agency with some yobbo who'd rough up one of our clients. I'm not sure they haven't done it once already. It's a war, Bill, and no mistake. So – ?'

Owen was feeling the full effects of the drinamyl now. He felt confident. Perhaps over-confident.

'I wouldn't do it for anybody else. I wish I'd never met you,' he said, and laughed.

'See you at the Horse and Saddle in Richmond tomorrow, then. There's a bit of a backlog of names to clear up. After that, it'll be easy – just a few now and again. Thanks a lot, Bill.'

Owen nodded. 'Seven o'clock?'

'About seven,' answered King, and slid quietly from the room.

He went back to his own office along the quiet corridor, and wrote out his letter of resignation. He gave no reason for his departure and offered no apology for its abruptness. Let them make their own guess. He knew they would, and that it would be correct.

Then he dialled the Sure Friendship number. It was 5.0 p.m. A soft voice answered. Mary Plummer had a soft voice, but it was not hers. He guessed it was Alice Caldwell. 'I'm afraid Mrs Plummer's out.'

'Will you give her a message?'

'Surely.'

'Tell her I've fixed up the contact I mentioned to her.'

'Contact? Where?'

'She'll know. But tell her I won't be able to reveal his name. It's a very delicate matter. She'll understand. I'll be in tomorrow.'

He did go into the agency office the next day. But by then his life had changed again.

CHAPTER FOUR

When King had left him, Owen sat staring at a very dull report from one of his narcotics squad sergeants. He was not interested in it. He was recalling a scene at breakfast that morning. Madge had swung round from the gas cooker, brought the frying pan over to the kitchen table where he was sitting, scooped out two fried eggs, a sausage, a slice of bacon and a piece of fried bread, and put them on the warmed plate in front of him.

'All that fried food'll give you a coronary,' she said cheerfully. 'What did you have for supper last night?' She had not spoken to him since the previous morning, because he had been out in the evening, having a meal with an informant, and had crept in after midnight and gone straight to bed, quietly, so as not to wake her.

He didn't reply.

She let him chomp his way through a couple of mouthfuls of food.

'What did you have for supper last night?' she had asked again.

He shook his head, with its strong black hair, going a little grey around the ears, fixed his liquid brown eyes helplessly on her own black button eyes, and licked his full lips. He looked like a guilty schoolboy who had not done his homework.

'Oh, I don't know. Something. Quite enough.'

She had swung back to the cooker and banged the pan impatiently on to one of the gas rings. 'What?' she snapped.

'I can't remember.'

'Of course you can remember what you had to eat last night!'

He shook his head again. 'Well, I can't. What's it matter?'

She pulled out the grill and removed a slice of toast. It was hot and she flung it hastily on to the table beside him. 'You often say you can't remember what you had for supper the night before. What's the matter with you? You need a holiday, boy.'

Owen let his knife and fork drop down on to his plate with a clatter. 'There's nothing wrong with me, Madge. You think I'm suffering from amnesia or something?'

'I'm not suggesting anything, love. But it's funny you can't remember what you had for supper sometimes.'

He had attempted to smile, and said: 'Sometimes it's best forgotten, dear. Wonderful Mother Nature trying to help me.'

He picked up his knife and fork and began to saw through a sausage, but the smell of the fatty food had seeped up to him and made him feel queasy. He replaced the knife and fork on his plate, gently this time, and pushed the plate to one side.

'What's up, Bill? You sickening for something? 'Flu or something?'

He put his head in his hands and stared at the table-cloth.

'Nope. I'm not sickening for anything. I feel all right, really. I'm just not hungry.'

'Know what?'

He sighed and raised his head and said wearily:

'Yes, I know what you're going to say – that I need a holiday.'

'We could have a package-deal flip to Majorca, love. Couple of weeks, or ten days at least. You need to relax. Properly. Not just the odd day off now and then, like you had last year. Always on the end of the phone if they want you.'

He shook his head, stared at the uneaten food, picked up the sausage with his fingers, nibbled at it and put it down again.

'It's not easy, Madge. You know that.'

Madge had sniffed scornfully. 'Fat lot of good it's done you, being conscientious.'

'I'm a copper,' he muttered obstinately. 'Either you're a good copper or a dud copper, that's my view.'

Madge had been cooking herself a simple boiled egg. She turned away from him, scooped it out of the water with a wooden spoon and tipped it on to a tea-cloth to cool a little. She didn't like an egg so hot that you couldn't hold it.

'You're a good cop and a dedicated one, and a fat lot of good it's done you recently,' she repeated.

'Oh, well – perhaps next time round.'

She said nothing. She didn't need to. He knew she was thinking that with the current tendency to promote younger men to key positions there might not be another time soon. But he didn't feel as deeply about it as Madge did.

'If not, it'll be that bitch Laura King's fault,' Madge said fiercely. 'I'm going to give her a piece of my mind if you don't get promoted.'

'Laura's all right.'

Madge Owen gave a short, hard laugh. 'You wouldn't have thought so, the scornful way she looked at you that day at the picnic.'

'Oh, the picnic!'

'Yes, oh, the picnic.'

Bill Owen had nodded, then frowned. His pulse rate was quickening. He felt he was on the verge of a memory breakthrough, that the Formula 3 ingredient had indeed not worked. All he needed was a hint now. He took a gulp of tea and said:

'Madge, apart from the way she looked at me, did you notice anything else about Laura?'

'What?'

'That's what I'm asking; what, if anything?'

'You needn't put on your interrogation voice, Bill Owen. What might I have seen?'

'Anything, well, odd? Like as if she was – a danger?'

'A danger? Who to? Me? We had a little tiff, but – '

'Not you particularly, dear. You didn't feel any kind of other threat?'

'From her? What *kind* of threat?'

He hesitated. His pulse beat was nearly normal again. The prospects of a memory breakthrough were receding. In a way it was disappointing. But in a way it was a relief. He knew the memory would have been horrifying because the quick pulse rate had been accompanied by trembling. Now the trembling had eased. Only a fragment of the threatened recall remained, like a fetid smell from a horror-laden plague cart which has approached, paused, and then passed on.

'What threat?' snapped Madge again. 'For heaven's sake, Bill! What threat?'

'I just wondered – if you saw or felt anything.'

'Like from your precious parallel existence?' she sneered.

'Like from anywhere. Perhaps – '

'Perhaps what?'

He shrugged and took another sip of tea. 'Maybe to do with snakes.'

'Oh, you and your snakes! I defended you, but I felt downright ashamed of you, Bill Owen, yes I did! There was only one, and that was dead.'

'There were little ones.'

'Little ones! They were in a tree yards and yards away!'

'Forget it,' sighed Owen helplessly.

But she hadn't finished with him. She sat down opposite him, grasped a knife with her strong right hand and neatly sliced the top off her boiled egg. She was worrying at him like a dog with a ham bone. With her mouth full of boiled egg and toast, she said:

'Does it occur to you, you being a clever *dick*, so to speak, that the Commissioner might have heard about your – memory lapses, shall we call them? – from more than one source? And that that might be one reason why you may not get Harry King's job? Ever thought of that? If a man can't remember what he had for supper the night before – '

Her voice died away. If he missed promotion, her practical north country mind could find only one explantation: over-work and mental fatigue, and Laura King getting word to the top brass.

'Maybe the Commissioner will think you have enough on your plate already,' she added, 'if you can't remember simple things like meals.'

Owen thumped the table, not forcefully but gently, two or three times.

'Look, I did a test the other day. Wrote out from memory a report of a lengthy interrogation I'd done. Later, I compared it with a tape recording which I'd ordered to be made of the interview. I found I'd omitted nothing of importance. If something's important I remember it, see? What I had for supper isn't, so I sometimes don't. It's as simple as that.'

He pulled his plate back towards him, and began to prod the fried eggs and saw at the bacon. In the end he managed to swallow most of the food, forcing it down, largely because it would please Madge.

Sitting in his office recalling that morning's breakfast scene, he knew it wasn't as simple as Madge thought. He had had a bad trip the night before the breakfast confrontation, and Formula 3 had erased 90 per cent of it from his memory. But something remained. Something to do with snakes.

Owen totally abandoned his desk work, pushing the report aside to gaze thoughtfully at the office wall opposite him, and the girl in the fishing net.

Outside, the day was drawing in. He looked at his watch. It was nearly 5.30 p.m. Something, perhaps the drinamyl tablets, had cleared his mind; and the remains of the trip suddenly made sense. Now, with brilliant clarity, he saw that Harry King was in a bad way. Unbalanced. He must be, or he wouldn't have resigned so suddenly and joined the Sure Friendship Marriage firm, thought Bill Owen with his newly found percipience. Harry was obsessed by Buller's threat, despite his assumed nonchalance. He was afraid now of what Buller might do, though he had once affected not to be.

Owen remembered what King had said about the necessity to get rid of Buller; and his own words about six feet under the ground, or in the river. He sighed, hoping Harry wouldn't do anything silly.

And now, at last, he remembered the other thing, too. The thing he had almost glimpsed at the picnic. Perhaps Formula 3, shielding the memory, only worked for a short time anyway. He didn't know. All he did know, now, was that Harry needed protection. Harry was his friend. His very good friend. As good a friend as a man could wish for.

For a further few minutes Bill Owen sat at his desk, head in his hands, staring with his mind's eye. Suddenly he felt the beginning of the turmoil in his nerve centres, in his stomach, which he knew heralded the onset of the impossible dream. Always before he had switched off, pushed the subject from his mind because it involved the ultimate betrayal. But now, he let it flood over him.

Would it be betrayal or an act of mercy?

On the way out, he put his head round Harry King's door. King was going through old papers in a desk drawer.

'Coming my way, Harry?'

63

King shook his head. 'I'd hoped to get back early, but I might as well start clearing up all this muck.'

'I'll wait on a bit, if you like. We could have a drink at the Station.'

'Don't bother, Bill; I'll be another couple of hours, perhaps more.'

'Fair enough. I'll see you tomorrow, then.'

'See you tomorrow, Bill.'

So be it, Owen thought as he left the building. Somebody or something in Parallel Existence had decided things for him. Yet he went on his way with a heavy heart, for he was dreading the evening.

Madge was wrong about Laura King. Quite wrong.

But she didn't know how wrong she was, he thought, because she refused to believe in Parallel Existence – that all around us were people and civilisations from other ages. To avoid disorientation Mother Nature had insulated us from them. But you could get through if you were a hermit – or with the aid of certain drugs. Madge said it was 'all bosh'.

He himself knew for certain, now, how wrong Madge was, and why; and the knowledge sickened him.

CHAPTER FIVE

Harry King often said that people tried to force significance into coincidence. With the benefit of hindsight they consult the zodiac and the stars in general, say, 'Ho-hum!' and add that any fool could have seen that something like that would happen.

Nothing good, they might have said, could happen to Laura King on 29 October. Laura, for one, believed in such things, and had noted that the stars column in the previous day's evening newspaper had said the following day would be a trying one for her.

When it started badly, she was not surprised. The newspapers arrived late, and the milk did not arrive at all. The vacuum-cleaner jammed, and the hose in the washing-machine went adrift so that water flooded the kitchen floor. And after lunch Madge had phoned, asking herself to tea at four o'clock. Her voice was tinny. She would be difficult. Laura guessed she had heard Bill Owen's bad news. Perhaps he had thought it prudent to warn her by phone.

Madge would recall the row at the picnic. Madge would think Harry had not done his best for Bill. Madge might blame her, accuse her of influencing Harry. Laura sighed. She had passed Madge that morning, and Madge had been wearing an unbecoming grey trouser suit, and her long shapeless grey overcoat which would have looked better on Harry. In fact, Harry had one rather like it. But then poor Madge never did dress well, thought Laura happily.

But Madge would be difficult. Certainly. And she was.

In the garden the frost seemed to have nipped the little magnolia tree of which Laura was so proud. And one of the two electric bulbs in the hall had burned itself out with a flicker and a faint metallic click.

Some days are so filled with minor disasters that they have a black humour about them, and she looked forward to recounting to Harry the things that had happened since he had left in the morning; knowing that, with a philosophical male attitude towards small domestic misfortunes, he would probably say, 'well, well, we live in a stirring age', and kiss her, and she would pretend to be indignant until he had kissed her for the second time. He always kissed her twice, once on arrival, and a second time later, on any convenient pretext. This time the excuse would be that he was sympathising with her on account of all the day's troubles.

Madge had not stayed long: little more than half an hour. She had not directly accused Laura or Harry of sabotaging Bill's promotion, but had contented herself with bitter remarks on lack of appreciation for good work, and a vague ambiguous comment about finding out one's true friends in difficult times. Her black eyes had moved restlessly as she gazed around, as though she had never seen the place before and was trying to memorise the position of doors and windows.

Then she had glanced at her watch and said that she

must be going, that she would 'be in touch', and that they must meet again soon 'despite what had happened'. It had been an icy and, with its undertone of reproach, an unfriendly meeting. But it could have been worse, thought Laura. Much worse. She closed the front door after Madge with a sigh of relief.

Harry did not usually come home until about 7.45, so she had been delighted that morning when he had said he would probably be back earlier than usual.

She heard the door bell ring and knew she had to let him in. He could not let himself in with only his key, because at his insistence she kept the chain on after dark. She had a strong suspicion that, although he maintained it was only for general security reasons, it was in fact due to his fear of Fred Buller and what Buller might do, even though he had affected not to fear Buller. She, too, feared the big bulking Buller. She had been scared stiff when she had seen him in the street.

She was about to shout, 'Coming, darling!' but changed her mind, and instead of tap-tapping in her neat brown shoes from the living-room into the short passage that led to the hall and door, she removed her shoes, put them down in the living-room and walked noiselessly to the door, having evolved a crude little practical joke based on the *Mary Celeste* mystery.

She would push the mat against the door so that the door would not open easily, turn the Yale type lock and fix it with the snib so that he could push it open, and then slide the chain along; then, but for a temporary difficulty due to the mat, he could enter. Meanwhile, she would have skittered out of the passage and hidden herself upstairs.

In the living-room he would find her shoes, and a half-finished cup of tea, still warm. But not her.

After he had called her name once or twice she would come downstairs and look innocent and surprised, and say, 'Can I get you anything, sir?' And he would probably say, 'Yes, you can bring me a kiss.'

It would be childish but fun, spur-of-the-moment moment fun, the sort of fun she liked – and which he liked, in spite of the lugubrious look he sometimes had when his face was in repose.

But it misfired because the mat had not been so obstructive as she had thought it would be, and she heard the scrape as the door opened when she was hardly out of the hall.

In fact, she was still partly in the hall when she decided to call it all off, and turned to greet him with a smile and saw the figure with a stocking over its head and screamed: 'Harry, stop it, take that stocking off, it's not funny, it's not funny!' She was vaguely aware of a grey coat and grey trousers.

Then it was on her.

Assuming it was a man, she screamed that he could take anything he liked, but it made no difference.

Although she was a slight woman, fear and desperation sent the adrenalin pumping vigorously. Once she broke away, nearly reached the front door, and called 'Harry!' twice, as she had called his name on two perilous occasions before in her life. Once, when some burning fat had set light to a tea-cloth which had set light to a broom handle, and her apron had caught as she tried to extinguish the fire; and Harry had rushed in and thrown her to the ground and rolled her in a kitchen mat. And once when she had got into difficulties when swimming off the Cornish coast, and Harry, a strong swimmer, had grabbed a mixture of hair and bathing cap and dragged her back to shore.

She called his name in fear for the third time in her life; three is supposed to be a lucky number, and she felt sure he would plunge through the front door – or perhaps the sound of his running feet on the garden path would be enough.

But the only sound she heard was the noise of the telephone bell ringing, and despite her struggles she had a fleeting but correct thought that it might be Harry ringing up to say he would, after all, be a little later than expected.

Then the fight went out of her.

She became limp, and the attacker was able to do what the attacker wished, which had nothing to do with rape or robbery. Harry King surmised that later. He guessed it from the slashes and bruises on her face, neck and head – and something else: the attacker had hacked off her hair, and most of the lovely, wavy, light tresses lay around her head on the floor.

But she was still alive. He knew enough about First Aid not to try to do anything for her except gently place a cushion under her head, gritting his teeth and stifling his sobs of despair and rage – and of self-reproach because he had not taken seriously enough what Bill Owen and Laura herself had tried to express: that Buller was not just a big mouth. But what could have been done to protect her? An indefinite twenty-four-hour guard on her was impossible. The fact remained that he, a copper, had not been able to protect his own wife.

As she lay face downwards in the hall, the wooden floor beneath her and around her was stained and sticky, and sprinkled with her hair. In the living-room, Harry found her shoes, and the half-finished cup of tea. It was cold now. He waited for the ambulance, and for the police.

After leaving the hospital, where Laura still lay unconscious, he spent the night with a colleague, Superintendent Robert Harper.

Mentally and physically in a state of shock, numbed and cold, he let the goose flesh come and go as it pleased; doing little about the cold, because nothing could be done – because the ice was inside him, trying protectively to numb his brain. And in some measure succeeding, which was just as well; neither fire nor alcohol nor strong sweet tea seemed able to reach it.

The motor had frozen up solid.

Later, he wondered if the Sleeping Beauty had been put into her long, long sleep by some devastating shock such as he had suffered.

The motor remained frozen up all the next day, and all the next night; then it coughed, spluttered, and began to tick over, slowly at first, but with gathering speed. It was drinking up a new fuel, one that Harry had not used before – and did not, at first, recognise because he had hitherto enjoyed an equable nature.

The first clue to the nature of the fuel came when by chance something, some mention of Rome and Romans, recalled the time, an eternity ago, when as a boy he had played Mark Antony in *Julius Caesar* at school; after the murder of Caesar he had shouted menacingly the lines, 'And Caesar's spirit, ranging for revenge, With Ate by his side, come hot from hell, Shall in these confines with a monarch's voice Cry "Havoc" and let slip the dogs of war, That this foul deed shall smell above the earth With carrion men groaning for burial.'

The quotation didn't fit, because Laura was not a monarch, and he himself wouldn't recognise Ate if he saw him, and no dogs of war were available. But Harry King guessed the motor which kept him going was fuelled by hate.

He was happy with hate, because it helped to take his mind off his misery.

Superintendent Harper used the machinery at his disposal to the best advantage. Detectives questioned everybody known to Harry and Laura King. Everybody except the one person Harper wished to interrogate.

Frederick Buller had disappeared.

His business partner, Ernest Dicker, claimed to know nothing of his movements. Pressed by Harper, fat Dicker shook his head, jowls wobbling.

'He just left a note saying he was going to the Continent on bureau business. Maybe to Holland. Said he'd be in touch. He hasn't been. Maybe he's picked up a floozy.'

'I don't believe you,' Harper said.

'Too bad,' Dicker said smoothly. 'That's just too bad, isn't it?'

Harper sighed, returned to the questioning, and got nowhere. He gave up. Dicker was not the sort who would respond to a little bouncing around. Dicker would be on to his lawyer, Bauer, in two minutes; and Bauer would have to do something. Dicker was a bigger fish than his partner. Before long, Harper meant to land him too.

Nobody guessed that benevolent ex-Superintendent Harry King was capable of real hatred, let alone hatred of such intensity that he came to refer to it to himself as 'the red mist affliction'. That was on the occasions when it flooded over him in waves which came near to rendering him unable to speak coherently or act normally.

There was no question of what is sometimes called an apoplectic rage. He could usually control the inner trembling which accompanied an attack, and veil the expression in his eyes until the worst had passed. Yet the hatred never left him. It was a matter of intensity. There were short periods when he felt comparatively calm; but most of the time he was conscious of it, gnawing at his stomach like a rat, or giving him a sharp pain in the midriff like a duodenal ulcer.

At one time he thought he might be developing such an ulcer. He was not. There was only the hatred. Controllable, though when the red mist came it was never easy to disperse.

He had had a foretaste of the red mist affliction during his visit to Mary Plummer. But then it had been aroused by the mere possibility of an attack on Laura. Now it was different. Now it was not just a possibility. The horror had happened.

People did not suspect hatred when he was afflicted, because there was never any apparent reason to suspect anything except the after effect of shock. It was not triggered off by a quarrel, an insult, a clumsy knock or other physical action. He kept his hatred secret and nurtured it. Apart from certain obvious things, such as a news item about a killing, he was himself often taken by surprise at the sort of sparks which could ignite an inner emotional explosion.

A headline in a newspaper could bring on an attack, or a chance spoken sentence about something which did not in itself concern him; or an advertisement for life insurance; or an advertisement in an Underground train showing a happy young couple about to take possession of their first house, apparently dazed for joy; or, on television, another young couple, astonished at the cheapness of some furniture they wished to buy, and at the easy-payment terms – sometimes looking not only surprised but bemused, if not indeed downright half-witted.

The red mist only remained a few seconds.

In point of fact, although he thought of it as red, it was usually more pink than red. If it had been possible to vaporise the stuff he would have been inclined to think of it as diluted and vaporised blood, which for a while tinted everything he looked at, both living and inanimate.

Then it was gone, and only the hate remained.

With his colourless, undramatic appearance Harry King could have been likened to a slumbering grey volcano. Around and about, the peasants tilled the fertile soil and obtained their three crops a year, deceived by quiescence, unaware of the seething danger in their midst.

Even Superintendent Harper had had no inkling of it. He had always thought of King as very quiet and soft – too soft, when it came to interrogations. Once he had said: 'You want to push 'em around a bit.'

'Not if you want the truth,' King had replied. 'A man will say anything under torture – some will, anyway. They'll say yes, yes, yes, or no, no, no – yes, sir, no, sir, three bags full, sir, just stop what you're doing, sir. Then you're left with a proper old mess, then you've got to spend a lot of time and effort trying to sort out the truths, the near-truths, and the I'll-say-anything untruths – if you can, that is.'

Harper had still not been convinced. He still thought King too soft. Nice bloke. But a bit squeamish.

He had no idea of the rage and cruelty to which, in certain conditions, King might willingly surrender himself – and which, one day, he would long for and plan for.

Nor had his wife Laura ever guessed it.

After twenty years of happy marriage, she had said more than once, she had never known him lose his temper; get a bit crotchety, yes, but not lose his self-control in any way, or do an unkind act, or say a hurtful, vicious thing to man, woman, or child. She would have sworn on oath that there was no sleeping volcano of hate inside Harry King, and never could be.

This was ironic, since she was the cause of awakening it, involuntarily – and unwillingly: for even when the hidden fire was beyond control and the white-hot lava had started on its trail of destruction, she did her best

74

to minimise what she feared could be fatal damage to her beloved Harry. It was too late; he had to take his calculated risk. But she tried. A few hours after the attack, as she lay critically ill in hospital, in a rare moment of consciousness when Harry King was sitting by her bedside, she opened her eyes and whispered: 'No revenge, darling. Too dangerous, my love – promise? It was – '

'Don't worry, sweetheart,' he murmured evasively, and pressed her limp hand. She did not hear his words because she had fallen asleep again before she could complete her sentence. The house surgeon was embarrassed and evasive when King questioned him about her. 'The longer she can hang on the better. We're doing our best.' The usual non-committal stuff, he thought, and went downstairs. Then he saw the flowers on the reception desk.

The intelligent young brunette receptionist had signalled to him as he was on his way out, and pushed the red roses towards him. He took them; he thought they might have come from Bill Owen. But there was no indication as to who they were from. Only a typed card: 'So sorry about your misfortune, dear. Heard about it on the radio.'

Something about the words rang a faint bell. Then he remembered being irritated because Buller had so often called Mary Plummer 'dear'. Mechanically, meaninglessly.

'Who left these flowers?' he asked.

'Tall gentleman with a pale face and black eyes. Didn't leave a name.'

She turned back to some accounts she was sorting,

then looked up and said: 'He asked if Mrs King was alone; if so, could he take the flowers up himself, she might like a visitor. I said, course she's alone, she's very ill and can't see anybody except her husband, and only him for a few minutes.'

'Correct,' said Harry King. 'Keep it that way as long as she's here. Understand?'

She seemed surprised at the hard tone of his voice, but she nodded. 'How long will she be here, sir?'

Her grey, thoughtful eyes searched his face. They were expressionless, and just because they were blank he guessed the question they were trying to conceal. What she meant was 'How long will she be here and not in a morgue?'

'Who knows? I don't. Nor do the doctors.'

He had lifted the roses up and was holding them at arm's length. There must have been two dozen of them. An expensive job. Then he laid them down gently, waiting for the swirling red mist to disperse.

'You all right, sir?'

'Quite all right.' He pointed to the roses. 'They gave me a funny feeling; they've been made up in an odd way. They would be a nice bouquet. But they look a bit like a funeral tribute – one of those sheaf arrangements people sometimes send instead of a wreath, don't they? Don't you think so?'

He was calm again now.

The receptionist laughed awkwardly. 'Oh, I'm sure the gentleman didn't mean it that way!'

'Not kind of hedging his bets? Backing things both ways? Ordering what you might call a dual-purpose make-up?'

'That's cynical, sir.'

'Not cynical. Just assessing the possibilities. I'm a police officer, or was. We do that. It becomes a habit.'

He had taken out his pocket knife and ripped the paper off the roses and cut the bindings which kept the flowers in place, and gone through the flowers, stem by stem, laying them on the desk in front of him. He didn't know what he expected to find hidden in them, and he found nothing.

'Shall I put a bit of string round them, sir, and send them up to Mrs King, looking just like an ordinary bunch?'

'No. Give them to somebody else. Or keep them yourself. Or put them in a vase for one of the wards.'

When she looked doubtful, he added: 'She doesn't like red flowers. Not even roses.'

'All right, Mr King.'

'And don't let anybody go up and see her, even if the doctor says she can have visitors. Especially not *him*. She doesn't like him. It might give her a set-back. Understand?'

She nodded again and watched him go out, her eyes still expressionless. He knew what she was thinking. She wore a wedding ring, and she would tell her husband that evening about an over-jealous man who would not let his wife have red roses from another man, and you met all sorts in a hospital, didn't you?

He walked slowly away from the hospital. Even if it had been Buller who had sent the flowers, there was nothing illegal about it. Maybe it was Buller, maybe not; there were plenty of people who were tall, dark, and had black eyes. If it was Buller – then so what? Nothing illegal, nothing illegal.

At the end of the road he looked back at the hospital, thinking of his Lauralie with her hair shorn and her head swathed in bandages, hoping desperately she could hang on. Shy by nature, and undemonstrative, he wished that he had been able to show her how much he loved her. He thought that she guessed it. But guessing is one thing, hearing the words spoken aloud is another and more substantial satisfaction. He vowed that in future, if there were a future for her, he would overcome his shyness with her. Never again would she have to scheme to be kissed twice when he returned from work.

He knew he lacked what is generally known as leadership, had only progressed professionally by a strict attention to detail, by luck, and by keeping a lower profile than Bill Owen did. That was in the past now. But at least he could be warmer and less shy with Laura. He swallowed twice, shook his head, and went back the following day to the agency. Mary Plummer needed protection, too. What little he could give, he thought bitterly, after thanking her for her sympathy.

One of the first things he did was to ask her for Alice Caldwell's address and telephone number. Mary Plummer pointed to one of the card index boxes.

'It's in there,' she replied indifferently. Then, head on one side, she watched him flick through the cards, and write Alice's address and phone number in his diary.

'She's married,' Mary Plummer said.

'And I'm old enough to be her father, and my wife is – ' He did not finish the sentence.

'Sorry,' said Mary contritely.

'Forget it, Mary, forget it. I like to have home addresses and phone numbers – just in case. I haven't got yours, incidentally.'

'It's in the same box. Under "P" for Plummer, in case you've forgotten.'

King's grey face creased in a smile. Mary could be sharp, if not indeed downright tart, when she wanted to be, he thought with approval. He liked people with a cutting edge which was normally shielded, as his own was.

At lunchtime he forced himself to eat a ham sandwich and drink a glass of beer in a pub round the corner. He was back in the office in three quarters of an hour, and found a note on his desk in Mary Plummer's handwriting:

The hospital phoned while you were out and left a message. The gist was that regretfully there was no longer any real reason to visit the hospital, and has not been since 12 noon. I hate to be the one to tell you this, and can only bring myself to do so in writing.

Mary.

He put the piece of paper down on his desk and drew in his breath. He re-read it. Then he crumpled it up and tossed it into the wastepaper basket.

Inside him the lava of hatred bubbled and swirled to

its peak. He sat down and waited till the red mist had cleared from his brain.

Then he put on his overcoat and went out. He passed Mary Plummer, standing tight-lipped and white-faced in the passage.

'Thank you for the note,' he said politely. 'I suppose it's just one of those things that happen,' he added inanely, and pushed past her.

'You'll want some time off, Harry – '

'Compassionate leave?'

She nodded. He shook his head.

'Compassion and I have nothing in common. Nothing at all.'

'Don't do anything silly, Harry.'

'I won't – that's for sure.'

He already had his rough plan for the killing of Buller. Laura's death would merely accelerate the preliminary work. Only Frederick Buller's quick and violent murder, that and the planning of it – especially the planning – would save his sanity. Laura would understand that now. But in deference to her, and to his own professional pride, it had to be a one-hundred-per-cent-secure job. That required a cool brain.

Harry King's brain was not cool when he left the office. But later that day, he again recognised reluctantly that hatred and the thought of revenge could have a beneficial spin-off. Certainly they occupied his mind sufficiently to enable him to ride out the first devastating shock of Laura's death and to attain an equilibrium which was shrouded in ice-cold malignity.

He realised that the bubbling lava had solidified into a terrifying amalgam: one which would enable him to think clearly and, when the opportunity arose, to kill with precision and safety. How and when he did not yet know. But he was a very dangerous man.

He had been speaking the truth when he had told Mary that he and compassion had nothing in common, and he gloried in the knowledge that no shred of social conscience would now weaken his resolve to murder Buller.

CHAPTER SIX

Good detectives have hunches. Some pay off, some don't. King had been a good detective, and he had a hunch; no sight of a great blazing trail, but faint indications such as an American Indian might note – like a blade of flattened grass, a snapped-off twig, a hair or two caught and held by the rough bark of a tree.

It was less even than that; it was a poor, weak, wispy hunch, but it held him as the fine web of a spider will hold a big fly. As the fly struggles, so King struggled, and as the fly gives up in the end, so did King: he knew that he must test the hunch.

When he left the office that evening he took a taxi to a big toy shop in Regent Street, and browsed for a while among the woolly Teddy bears, floppy dogs, and unlikely-looking rabbits. Finally he selected a bear about eighteen inches tall wearing a blue limp sunhat, in which two holes had been made so that the ears poked through.

He had it gift-wrapped in bright jazzy paper, asked for a card, and wrote on it, 'Happy Birthday – a little late – to Lucy from your affectionate Uncle Harry.' If his hunch were right, the card didn't matter; if it were wrong, it would just cause some bewilderment, even pleasure, and that wouldn't matter either.

Clutching the bear, he took a taxi to Pimlico, asked in a tobacconist's shop where the school was, and stopped the taxi about a hundred yards from the kindergarten. The little side street was deserted. He stood outside a square Victorian house.

The front door bell was answered by a young, buxom, blonde woman dressed in some uniform to imply that she was a trained children's nurse, fully competent to cope with anything from cuts and bruises to tears and tantrums.

'It was little Lucy Caldwell's birthday recently,' King said. His smile was almost a grimace. 'Could you give her this Teddy bear? You know what kids are – they think they shouldn't go to school on their birthdays, but I think Lucy did. This is to show her that little girls who are good on their birthdays and go to school sometimes get nice surprises,' he added, and felt a little sick at his nauseating words.

'Come again? What's the kid's name?'

'Lucy Caldwell.'

He thought she was probably Australian from her accent and her independent manner.

'Just a minute.'

She turned and went indoors, leaving him on the doorstep. After a while she returned and said:

'There's no kid called Lucy Caldwell comes here, an' nobody with a name like it, neither.'

King nodded, thinking fast, thinking it figured with the idea he had in mind about Alice Caldwell, and her late arrivals at the office.

'Here, give this to some other kid; I must've got it wrong. I'm going to America tomorrow, anyway. It's no good to me. New York Customs would probably rip it open to see if it was stuffed with heroin. Go on, take it.'

He thrust the bear at her. She took it, smiled and said pertly,

'Might keep it myself.'

'That's up to you.'

'Thanks.' She took the toy, smiled again, and closed the door.

King walked back to Orange Square, went into one of the phone boxes there and telephoned Owen at the Yard.

Owen answered. 'Oh, it's you, Harry. I hope you haven't been trying to get me.'

'No – why?'

'I didn't come in yesterday. Took the day off. For once in my life I couldn't face the grindstone.'

Clearly, Bill Owen hadn't heard about Laura. King didn't feel like telling him. 'Listen, Bill, can I see you tomorrow? Usual time and place?'

'Sure,' agreed Owen.

'Meanwhile, have you got any spare youngsters in need of a spot of tailing practice?'

There was silence. He could imagine Bill Owen turning the question over in his mind, brown eyes thoughtful, suspecting a long and laborious job for two of his men.

'Not many,' Owen said cautiously. 'Why?'

'Can't tell you on the phone. Got a pencil?'

'Okay.'

'Alice Caldwell, 427 Ebury Street, S.W. Probably leaves home around eight in the morning, possibly with a kid, possibly not. Might go to a kids' nursery school, might not. Will end up at my office. At which point call off surveillance.' He paused, then added in a wheedling tone: 'Matter of a couple of hours, Bill. Can do?'

There was another, longer silence. Then Owen said:

'Can do. Shouldn't, without more info. But will do – for you. I'll call it a training exercise. Harper will have a copy of the result.'

'That's okay, but you needn't tell him it's for me.'

There was a short silence.

'All right,' Owen said, with a tinge of reluctance.

'Thanks. Be seeing you.'

King replaced the receiver and smiled contentedly.

Nothing dramatic had resulted from passing the Sure Friendship agency names over the C.R.O. records via Bill Owen. Two clients had committed car offences – driving with too much alcohol in their blood – and there was one case of shop-lifting. Otherwise nothing.

He had told Mary Plummer about what he called his 'indirect access' to the C.R.O., but had mentioned no names. The old police instinct not to reveal the name of an informant or delicate contact was still strong in him. Shrewdly she guessed this, and did not question him.

Now, the day after his phone call to Bill Owen, he sat in the Richmond pub shortly after opening time eager to see if his hunch were correct. He had bought two pints of beer, so that Bill's would be ready for him when he arrived. Punctually at six fifteen Bill Owen pushed open the saloon bar door and came over to him.

'I just want to say – ' Owen began, in a low voice.

'Don't,' interrupted Harry King. 'Please don't.'

'Okay, Harry, I won't. They told me at the office.'

There was something about Bill Owen's sympathy that King knew he would not be able to stand.

Owen had put two young detectives on the tailing job, and had their report with him. It read:

ALICE CALDWELL

Subject A left home at 8.10 a.m. alone and proceeded on foot to Sloane Square. Here subject stopped for some minutes on the south side, apparently looking for a taxi. Finally subject took a bus up Sloane Street in a northern direction, alighted at Hyde Park Corner bus stop, and continued on foot to the Hilton Hotel. A considerable number of tourists were arriving, and for some three or four minutes she was lost to us.

Subsequently she was observed sitting on a settee having a cup of coffee with a male (subject B).

They were observed to be conversing in what seemed a confidential manner. At five minutes past ten, Subject A left the hotel. It was considered wise to divide the surveillance team. I followed Subject A.

Subject B seemed to be aged between forty and forty-five, short, stout, height about 5 ft. 5 ins., large stomach, otherwise squarely built, with the remains of blond hair, small blue eyes, and a pink complexion. He was dressed in a blue mohair suit, and wore a blue tie. He frequently used a gold toothpick, and was smoking a cigar during the time he was under observation. He appeared to be on friendly terms with Subject A, and for part of the time kept his left hand on her knee; but no improper advances were observed, nor did Subject

A appear to resent his advances, if such they were.

Detective Constable Smith continued observation on Subject B until he left the lounge at 10.05 a.m. after the departure of Subject A.

Subject B was observed to make certain notes in a small brown notebook. He spoke to nobody while in the lounge except Subject A. Subject B on leaving the lounge took a lift, possibly to his room.

D.C. Smith did not attempt to enter the lift with him, but from discreet enquiries made states that Subject B may be a British subject, Ernest Dicker, who booked in at the hotel from Liverpool two weeks ago.

Subject A proceeded by bus to Fleet Street. On two occasions during the journey she took from her handbag a large white envelope and held it up to the light. On one occasion she also took a slim pencil from her bag and applied it to one end of the envelope, possibly with some idea of attempting a dry-opening, but she apparently thought better of it.

At a small office building in Blackfriars Court, occupied by legal firms, she examined the names in the hall and placed the envelope in the letter box of an office of which the tenants were A. Bauer & Co., Solicitors.

She then hailed a taxi and, no other taxi being available, surveillance had to be discontinued.

Descriptions: Subject A known to you.
Subject B as above.

King handed the report back to Owen, who sniffed and wrinkled his nose and said: 'There are gaps, of course. It doesn't say if the woman returned direct to your office, or when.'

88

'It'll do,' interrupted King. 'It's about what I expected.'

Owen said: 'I had a few other enquiries made in the C.R.O. Ernest Dicker has two or three convictions for con tricks, but way back, way back.'

'Nothing recent at all?'

'Marginal traces of drug connections in the Buller case – nothing proved.'

Harry King's eyes were thoughtful, half-closed. 'That's where the Round Circle money comes from – the capital – and where it'll go,' he said. 'Meanwhile, expect a take-over of marriage bureaux, by persuasion or violence. Slow, gradual. Britain, then France, Germany, U.S.A. The world in the end? The Western world, anyway. I may be wrong, but that's the way I see it.'

Owen shook his head doubtfully, and stroked his black hair. 'Too big and complicated.'

King pressed on: 'Nothing's too big or complicated for that drug lot. They think big.'

He paused and looked at Owen, reflectively at first. But Owen noted how a change came over his face. It became as hard as grey granite. He sat still and rigid, his eyes seemingly fixed on Owen's. But Owen knew they were fixed on something else. Totally concentrated. Unblinking. So might a fox sit, seeing his prey on a distant mound. Motionless. Implacable. And Owen knew he was not thinking about drugs.

'Don't do it, Harry,' muttered Owen. 'Harper'll nick you, if you kill Buller. That's for sure.'

King slowly turned his gaze from Owen's face. 'He won't, Bill. Not the way I'll do it.'

'That old thing, the perfect murder! There's no such thing.'

'There is, you know,' Harry said dreamily. 'Oh, yes, there is. Harper'll never pin it on me.'

Harry King frowned, and changed the subject. 'Bill – Mary Plummer and I, we're grateful; we'd like to show it.'

'Forget it. It's good honest crime prevention.'

'No cash or cases of whisky. But what about a short package holiday? Maybe to Majorca. Ten days. You and Madge. You look as though you could do with a break.'

Owen shook his head. 'It's not on, Harry. Thanks, all the same.'

'Are you being fair to Madge?'

'Don't you drag *her* in,' Owen said uneasily, but the damage was done. He remembered Madge's words at the breakfast table about the need for a holiday. She had even mentioned Majorca.

Work was not the only reason why he had resisted her pressure. Money was also involved, or lack of it. *Was* he being fair to Madge?

'I'll think about it,' he muttered ungraciously.

'Good,' said the pallid fox, who had his own reasons for wanting Owen to accept. Even an old colleague was expendable now; even one in such a mess as Owen seemed to be.

Harry King went home and stood where he had found Laura lying in her congealed blood and shorn hair. Not in a pool of blood. Blood congeals in a few seconds unless there is water. It can be reactivated later, but it couldn't by the time he'd found her. He was astonished and shocked by his technical line of thought, and paused, staring down at the floor.

He heard a creak and thought there might be a door opening somewhere in the silent house, and he might hear the tap-tap-tap of light footsteps, and see Laura on the stairs. Laura's spirit, ranging for revenge with Ate by her side. Nonsense, he thought, remembering her words in hospital; not Laura's spirit – she was too gentle.

But he wasn't. Not gentle like Laura. Under the thin, inexpensive Indian rug in the hall, he knew the wooden floor would be still faintly stained, though the mark would no longer bear any resemblance to blood.

He whispered to himself: 'Blood will have blood, they say,' and so it should. He wouldn't sell the house till blood had had blood. And the sooner the better.

He was hanging up his coat when he saw a piece of paper in the letter cage. He took it out, and read the typewritten message:

Mr Dicker says to say he wants a chat this even-ing around nine-thirty, sharpish, as he has other business. Hilton Hotel. General Lounge. He'll be wearing a light blue tie, white shirt and socks.

The message was unsigned.

This was a stroke of luck. A plan was in his mind and he had to get to know Ernest Dicker. It was an essential part of the plan and it was better that an approach should come from Dicker rather than the other way round. He did not know what Dicker wanted, nor did he care at the moment. He looked at his wrist-watch, put on his coat again, went out and caught a bus to Park Lane. He went into the Hilton and soon spotted Dicker, with his dark blue mohair suit, white shirt and socks, and blue tie.

Harry King had had no preconceived ideas of what Ernest Dicker would be like. But he had guessed he couldn't be another Buller. One was enough – almost too many, unless kept in the background. Two would send prospective clients hurrying in the opposite direction. Buller was the hatchet man. Dicker must be softer, at least outwardly.

Within a minute of meeting Dicker, King knew he was right. The surveillance report had told him that Dicker was a short man, stoutly built. He also had heavy jowls and large white hands. Small blue eyes were set in a round, fat, rubicund face. His once fair hair had all gone now, except for a fringe round the ears.

No beauty, but King could imagine Dicker putting on a warm avuncular act when it was needed. Little blue eyes twinkling. Face creased in smiles. Great belly shaking when he laughed.

But at the moment he was not avuncular. He was brusque at first.

He raised a hand as King approached. He didn't get to his feet. Instead he patted the seat on the settee beside him.

'You Mr Harry King?'

'I am.'

'Ernie Dicker.'

Dicker's voice was soft. King wondered whether the cinema and television copy life or whether life copies television and the cinema. King thought he must have been a menace even as a baby, and had never improved. The sort of fat, jolly baby whom visitors adored until his face suddenly went pink with rage and he tossed his food to the ground, if not into a visitor's lap.

Dicker's lips were thick; the nose thick, too, though straight.

Dicker was probably very dangerous, like many who were ruthlessly clawing their way to the top. King guessed that Dicker hadn't reached the top, but that he was well on the way.

Dicker looked at Harry King and suddenly smiled and said:

'Want a drink? Scotch on the rocks or something?'

'Don't mind if I do.'

Dicker waved his hand at a passing waiter, who stopped passing, and took the order. King was envious. Some people got instant service.

He felt Dicker's hand slap down on the settee beside him, and heard Dicker say. 'Know what?'

'Know what what?'

'Know what I think, if a bloke says, "Don't mind if I do," I think, "Don't mind if you don't." But it's different with you. We've got interests that overlap, right?'

'Have we?'

'Should be pals, eh?'

'Should we?'

An understanding smile spread over Dicker's face; but then he flicked his left arm forward, glanced at his gold wristwatch, and said with unexpected formality:

'You got to excuse me, but I got to go soon, Mr King.'

'Nobody's stopping you, Mr Dicker.'

King noticed the drink which the waiter had put in front of him: he picked it up, said: 'Thanks for the drink,' downed it in one gulp, and made as if to get up.

'You don't want to think about things,' Ernie Dicker said.

'I do. Things like nature, and animals and birds marking out their own territory – and defending it to the death.'

Dicker leaned forward and at the same time glanced at King sideways. 'That's interesting, what you say there,' he said eagerly, and turned on the settee and stared at Harry King. 'But it's a wrong idea people have! Animals – wolves and dogs, and stuff like that – they don't fight to the death, not often. People think they do, but they don't, not often.'

He was talking rapidly, blue eyes alight, with unexpected enthusiasm like that of a nature-lover.

'The loser turns aside,' he went on. 'He exposes his jugular vein to his opponent, sort of saying, "Okay, I give in, kill me if you want to, but I give in." Or he rolls on his back with his four paws in the air, meaning, "I surrender, I surrender." And the winner walks away, looking disapproving, like saying, "Well, that's that, and don't let's have any more trouble with you. You're not in my league." I reckon you're as sensible as animals, Mr King: yes, I do. I reckon you are.'

'I wouldn't know how to roll on my back with my four paws in the air, Mr Dicker,' he said softly.

'Are you speaking for this Plummer lady?'

94

'Yes, I think I am.' King paused. 'Well, that's that. You've got to go, I've got to go.' He again made to get up from the settee. It was risky, because Dicker might have let him go, which he didn't want. On the other hand, it would be wrong, unnatural, to become too friendly too fast.

He was pleased when Dicker pushed him gently back on to the settee. Dicker said, 'In the temporary absence of Mr Buller I thought that you and I – '

'Where is he?'

'On the Continent.' Dicker looked at him blandly, enquiringly.

Then he went on. 'You and me could be pals. It'd make sense,' he said.

He took a gold toothpick out of his pocket, did a little exploratory work on his front teeth, and put it back in his pocket.

'Shall I tell you something?'

'I'm not pressing you.'

Dicker nodded thoughtfully. He still seemed pre-occupied with his mouth. 'Trouble with these tooth-picks is they're too short,' he declared. But then he said:

'This Round Circle mob, they're rough.'

'You should know,' said King mildly.

Dicker blinked, creased his chubby face. His big stomach quivered, and he produced a sound like an infant gurgle.

'I try to control them, of course.'

'Of course.'

'But I can't be there all the time.'

'We'll get by, the Sure Friendship agency,' King murmured.

'I wouldn't gamble on it. But I could help you. I got my boys.'

King gave a cold smile. 'I know. I think there's a couple sitting on our right.'

Dicker ignored the remark. 'You'd get one-hundred-per-cent protection. Cheap at twice the price, I'd say.'

'Depends what the price is.'

Dicker waved a dimpled hand vaguely, in front of his own face, and said: 'We got to work that out. But first we got to agree in general.'

Harry King said nothing. He was trying to think things through, to explain two contradictions, as Mary had tried.

Dicker had invested money in the Round Circle agency. It would be in his interests to smash the Sure Friendship Agency. Yet Dicker was trying to extort protection money to keep the Sure Friendship firm in business. It didn't make sense. Or did it?

'Well?' asked Dicker, looking at his wristwatch again.

'I'm thinking,' King said truthfully.

Did Dicker feel that it would be better financially to 'protect' the Sure Friendship firm for a fee, even if it meant that the Round Circle crowd won fewer clients because the Sure Friendship Agency was still in existence?

The two agencies could probably exist – just – even in competition. The Round Circle would be making a profit from protection. But would the Sure Friendship survive if it had to pay out protection money? Would it in the end be glad to be taken over, at almost any price, by the Round Circle? And once protection cash could no longer be afforded, Round Circle, by one means or another, would know enough about its rival to render the final sabotage operation both easy and very, very cheap.

'Come in with me, Mr King,' he heard Dicker say. 'There's good lolly in love – if you know how to organise things.'

'No go. No amalgamation. No protection – can't afford it.'

'Sure you can afford *not* to have it?' Dicker said.

Then he got to his feet. 'Let me know if you change your mind in the next two weeks. I'm moving to the Wargrove Hotel, Bloomsbury.'

He was staring dreamily over King's shoulder to the right as he adjusted his blue tie, taking a long time doing so. 'Hope this Mary Plummer keeps healthy. They're tough, the Round Circle lot.'

King too had risen to his feet.

'Say hello to the wife,' Dicker added casually.

'I have no wife,' King said.

Dicker snapped his short fingers, as if impatient with himself. 'I'm sorry. Mr Buller told me. Some thugs beat her up. Terrible – terrible.'

'And killed her,' King said through his teeth.

'Too bad,' Dicker muttered. 'Tell this Plummer lady, and any who help out in the bureau, to go easy after dark. So long. Be seeing you.'

'I doubt it,' whispered King. 'I doubt it very much.'

'Up to you.'

Dicker turned and left without a handshake. King made his way out of the lounge. The two young thugs were no longer there. Only crumpled cushions showed where they had been sitting.

Gangsters hot up the coppers. Killing hots them up even more.

Yet killing a copper's wife was not the action of a psycho. A psycho would find easier victims, like lonely women existing in bedsitters – like some of our clients, thought King morosely, on the way back by slow bus to what had been home and was now an empty shell.

He turned down the tree-lined road near East Sheen Avenue where his house stood – small, square, compact, surrounded by a square compact garden. He and Laura had found it ideal, the final dream; quiet, detached but not isolated. Police accommodation was good enough, and money-saving, but when the job came to an end so did the accommodation. You were out in the cold. The house had been the ultimate sanctuary.

Sanctuaries are supposed to be safe places. In some ways it had provided sanctuary. In other ways it had provided as much security as a slaughter house for a calf.

But King was preparing the ground well for the safe killing of Buller. Developments were promising.

CHAPTER SEVEN

Buller wasn't a psycho, King thought again, as he let himself into the house. Buller was just a predatory animal, humiliated at having been caught and sentenced to a stretch in prison; vicious and vengeful; nursing his hatred in the prison hothouse, feeding and watering it, waiting for the time when it could blossom in blood-stained glory.

The house was lonely, but he was getting accustomed to that. Anywhere was lonely. His only real companion was his hatred, as it might have been Buller's in prison.

But Buller had other interests: greed for money, yearning for power, lust for gang leadership: In King's own case, he had only one friend to keep him warm, night and day – the hate which grew rather than lessened, like some triffid, which, like a triffid, threatened to destroy him. He recognised that. He knew there was a physical threat, that all men in white hats did not always triumph over all men in black hats, that there were occasions when men in white hats got clobbered good and proper. It couldn't be helped.

He opened the living-room door and switched on the light, and saw the gaping hole where the television screen had been, and the shattered remains of it on the carpet, and the slashed settee and armchairs, the wrecked china ornaments from the mantelpiece above the fireplace, and the light blue carpet, stained with what could have been ink from the smashed writing desk near the window.

Upstairs, it was the same story in the bedroom he had shared with Laura. Slashed clothes in the wardrobe, slashed blankets in the bed. On the bedside table, where the framed photograph of Laura had been, there was nothing.

The photograph itself, with a jagged hole in the middle of it behind the splintered glass of the frame, lay on the floor by the table it had stood on.

He was staring at the slashed photo of Laura and the typed note saying, 'Next time it's you and Mary Plummer,' when he heard the noise down below. It was a metallic sound, disjointed and of no long duration, the sound a pile of saucepans and frying pans might make if upset.

He was still wearing his raincoat, with the Walther automatic and the knuckleduster both in the right hand pocket; both offensive weapons within the meaning of the Act – but here he was on safe ground, here he was on his own property. A man is entitled to defend himself and his property – using, admittedly, the minimum of violence needed to do so.

Maybe he wouldn't use the minimum of violence, maybe he'd use lots of it; but if it came to a Court case, and his word against that of an intruder already on the premises, he was willing to gamble on who'd win. The fact that the firearm was unlicensed would lead to trouble, and the age-old excuse, that it was just a 'war souvenir', would cut no ice; there'd be a fine and confiscation of the weapon. But what of that?

He paused at the top of the stairs, listening.

The house was totally quiet, without even the sound, real or imagined, of the light tap-tap of Laura's footsteps – which he still liked to think he had heard, and knew he hadn't. After some seconds he realised that he had not been breathing. He expelled some air from his lungs, and was turning to retrace his footsteps to the bedroom when he again heard, from down below, seemingly from the kitchen, the same metallic sound, briefer and less loud than before, as of a pot being overturned.

He pulled out the Walther, pushed the safety catch forward, padded down the short staircase and stopped outside the kitchen door. The light switch was on the left. He paused, flung the door open and switched on the main light in the ceiling, holding the automatic in his right hand. He cautiously looked round from the doorway, almost on hands and knees so as to present the minimum target and be in an unexpected position.

Circumstances being what they were, and his finger being on the trigger, he knew that he would have shot first and asked questions afterwards, had he not seen a black and white cat which he recognised as one called Timmy from two houses down the road.

The cupboard door where the pots and pans were kept was open, and pots and pans were in disarray on the floor. He and the cat stared at each other. The cat had come in through the back door, forced open by the wreckers. Had it regretted it? Sensing something violent, had it taken refuge in the cupboard?

King automatically went and pulled the back door

nearly shut, and began to walk across the kitchen to tidy up the cupboard. As he did so, the cat mewed and skittered past him and stood by the kitchen door, sometimes trying to pull it further open with one paw, sometimes kneading the mat with its two front paws.

He put his automatic on the kitchen table and pulled the door further open, just wide enough to let the cat out. It ran out a few feet, then stopped, turned and ran back, tail up and stiff.

He wondered what it had seen to make it change its mind, and wished he had not put the Walther on the table. He slipped his hand into his right raincoat pocket and his fingers into the knuckleduster which lay there. It was of aluminium, a useful but pleasantly light job which he had 'liberated' during a raid on a Displaced Persons camp in Germany after the war.

He opened the door wide and saw the two men on the threshold, one slightly behind the other, with stockings over their heads in accordance with modern trendy fashion among crooks.

He raised his left forearm to smother the blow from the blackjack, and simultaneously flung his right forearm, knuckleduster and all, behind the first man's forearm, grasping his own left wrist with his right hand, lunging forward and downwards, bearing down with his full weight, keeping his head tucked down so that his own and his enemy's heads and bodies were entangled, making it difficult for the second man to intervene if he were carrying a weapon.

He heard the first man gasp with pain and scream out a four-letter word as his arm and shoulder blade took the strain of the wrenching, and felt the man's body sag beneath his own; but he did not let the man fall away, and recovered his own balance in time to see the second man raise his right arm and to see the hand with a flick knife.

King was now, for a couple of seconds, using No. 1's body as a shield, holding it close to him, hearing the gasps and obscene words pouring from the man's mouth.

'Right,' he muttered, and as No. 2 closed and sought an opening to use his knife, King let the other man's body fall, and drew back his right arm, and took a short step forward, and struck and heard the crack as the knuckleduster connected with No. 2's jaw, and watched him stagger to his knees, left hand to a jaw which was in no healthy condition. It was a diabolical blow, but he was in a diabolical mood.

Stocking Head No. 1 still lay on the ground, nursing what was probably a dislocated arm or shoulder blade.

The other remained on his knees fumbling to get the stocking off his injured face. Both were gasping and swearing. King was breathing heavily, the result of the exertion and emotion, but part of the emotion was exultation at having partially revenged the smashing of Laura's framed photograph.

'Right,' he gasped. 'You can go to a hospital in Kingston – I suppose, if you don't mind answering a few questions when you get there. I can't hold you both myself. But the cops will be round in about five minutes. Get to hell out of here – small timers.'

He had in fact no intention of ringing the police. It was a private war and it was not the small mindless animals he was after.

He picked up the blackjack from the ground and walked back into the house and locked the door. He thought there could always be a use for a short black-jack.

Nothing had been stolen. Not that there was much to steal. But the few little silver ornaments in the house were untouched. Shortly before midnight he telephoned Mary Plummer, at her home, apologising for disturbing her.

'I'll be in a bit late tomorrow,' he said in a matter-of-fact voice. 'Got some clearing up to do.'

The flat normality of his voice combined with the very ordinary message and the lateness of the hour alerted her. She was as bright as a button about some things. They were on comradely Christian-name terms by now, though there was no emotional involvement. There couldn't be. His only love was his hate, and would be for some time; perhaps for ever. Mary Plummer said:

'Clearing up, Harry?'

'That's what I said.'

'Been making a mess?'

'Not me – other people.'

He could almost hear her brain going tick-tock-tick-tock. 'Like here – well, not here, but like in the office?'

'That's right.'

There was silence for a few seconds.

'And Mary – '

'What?'

'Take care.'

'I always do.'

'Take particular care. I've got an idea Phase Three has begun.'

'What's Phase Three?'

'Phase Three is you and me, that's what Phase Three could be. So take care.'

He heard her sigh and say: 'How? How take care? Against what?'

It was the sort of practical down-to-earth question he would expect her to ask, and he didn't know the answer.

'Well,' he said, and paused.

After a while he heard her voice. 'You nodding off or something? Making up a poem, cooking an early breakfast?'

'No, I'm not.'

'How do I take care?' she pressed him. 'How, how?'

'Just – use common sense, I suppose,' he said desperately.

'Thanks, that's useful.'

'Don't walk alone through ill-lit pedestrian subways, and if you have to walk along ill-lit streets after dark try and do so with other people. Keep with a crowd. Double-lock your front door and put the chain on.'

'You'd better take care *yourself*, Harry, lad. You're about the only friend I can talk freely to.'

'I don't know about myself, but I reckon I've taken care of somebody else. He's lying outside, with a broken jaw, I hope – yes, I *do* hope so. And another one isn't so happy.'

He edged away from the table on which the telephone stood, glanced out of the window and said:

'He *was* lying outside; he isn't now. I suppose his pal

has lugged him off, may he rot. May they both rot, if possible.'

'I'll get Alice Caldwell to call round about ten o'clock tomorrow,' she said. 'Give you a hand with the clearing up. She'll be late, of course, as usual.'

But Alice Caldwell apparently made a special effort; she was in time for the final tidying up and carting out to dustbins.

He thought, as he had thought before, that Alice Caldwell was a pretty woman, with her round face, pink and white complexion, and soft skin. This would probably wrinkle easily when she was older. But at present it was attractive and, with her china blue eyes, snub nose, fair hair, and slender figure, it added to a very feminine appearance.

She added to this appeal an ability to flatter and admire. Harry King, viewing her with clinical detachment, thought that her husband, said to be a young accountant somewhere in the City, probably had a hard job to keep her on the straight and narrow. If he could and did.

He gave her an edited version of what had happened in the house, and she switched on her charm machine – looking at him with wide eyes, her rosebud mouth just sufficiently open to show her white teeth.

'Gosh,' she said, 'just like on the telly. What was the idea?'

He gave her a further run-down of events, telling her about Ernie Dicker.

She was playing it cool; but now he saw how he could use her.

'Is he a *big* gangster?' she asked.

'He might be,' he said uncertainly.

'You said he had a couple of thugs with him at the Hilton and they left more or less when he did.'

'Signifies nothing much, except that he was taking precautions. Giving himself protection. Like he offered us. Or pretending to. Showing off. But Mary Plummer would be against protection, same as she's against amalgamation, being taken over – which is what it boils down to.'

Alice Caldwell again switched on the charm machine and asked, wide-eyed and innocent: 'Do you think she's right?'

King looked gloomy.

'I don't know. I thought so at first but now – I'm not so sure. I'm not at all sure.'

Alice Caldwell switched off the charm machine, and when she spoke there was a note of disappointment in her voice.

'The firm's not made of money. Are you going to duck out, Mr King?'

'I got on fairly well with Dicker – considering the circumstances,' he said defensively. 'I thought he was quite civilised – really – on the whole. I could get on all right with him, I think, if I had to. No problem.'

'Ducking out.'

It was not a question, rather a statement.

'If you like to put it that way. But it's not as simple as it seems. You've got to have common sense. Weigh the pros and cons. All that.'

'Protection costs money,' she said.

'So does having the office wrecked. So does losing

clients, getting a bad reputation, going bust. And I wouldn't like to see Mary roughed up.'

Alice Caldwell shook her head.

'What are you shaking your head about?'

'Nothing. Well, just – I wouldn't have thought it, that's all. No, I wouldn't; I wouldn't have thought you had a soft centre.'

He looked hurt, and was, but it was inevitable. He sniffed and said: 'There are a lot of things people wouldn't think about me.'

People would imagine he was just a simple cop, he thought. Nobody would imagine that he planned to use Ernie Dicker to kill or maim Fred Buller – preferably both: maim him first, then kill him. Nor would anybody imagine that unlike Mary Plummer he had always had suspicions about Alice Caldwell with her innocent blue eyes. Or that he planned to use her, too, to kill Buller.

She was his link with Dicker. She would report to Dicker that he was weakening in his support for Mary Plummer.

But it had to be done slowly and with caution. Dicker was no fool.

People thought that slow, deliberate old Harry King, who was inclined to blow his nose like a trumpeting elephant, was a nice straightforward bloke, as dependable as he was destitute of guile. But Fred Buller's Guardian Angel should now have been stirring uneasily. Instead of planing around, engine idling, he ought to have been stirring his wing stumps.

When Alice had finished vacuum cleaning the living-room, King said he could do the rest himself, and watched her go out of the front door on her way to the office. He thanked her.

'That's all right,' she said, in a tone of no great enthusiasm.

He went up to the bedroom, where the shattered photograph of Laura still lay by the bedside. The frame and photo were beyond repair, but the actual damage did not matter much. He had a duplicate print which he had intended taking to the office to stand on his desk. Now it could stay by his bed.

He did not mind the loss of the photo. It was the desecration which made the red mist return.

When he went to the office, Mary Plummer came into his room at once. He was not surprised. He guessed Alice had reported his words. He thought Alice Caldwell was gabby.

Mary spoke to him as Alice had done:

'I'm a bit surprised, Harry! I didn't think you had a soft centre. I'm sorry to talk like this in view of – '

She began tapping with her neatly manicured forefinger on the arm of the chair by the side of his desk, where she was sitting. She had her right leg crossed over her left, and in addition to the finger tapping he noted that her right foot was waving up and down. He guessed that these two signs of tension were her storm signals, and began to batten down his hatches.

'It's the thin edge of the wedge,' she went on. 'You know that, of course? I thought we'd more or less agreed about that, about not being taken over.'

'You agreed about it, Mary. I didn't say much.'

'This firm's not made of money, Harry King. It really isn't.'

He knew what she was getting at. She had pumped a lot of her own money into the firm, maybe most of her savings; the business had been building up nicely, and she wanted to keep her paw on it. He himself had a police pension of sorts. She hadn't. He understood, all right.

He found it difficult to resist the temptation to take her into his confidence, to defend himself, rehabilitate himself in her eyes, tell her that things were not as they seemed, that his loyalty to the Sure Friendship bureau was unshaken, that he was with her one hundred per cent. Furthermore, that having Buller killed was not his only aim. He planned to demolish Ernest Dicker, too, but in a different way and for a different reason. Buller for revenge; Dicker because, from the bureau's point of view, Dicker was much more dangerous. There could be no safety for the Sure Friendship bureau, or even for Mary, so long as Dicker was hovering in the wings.

He saw the disappointed and wounded look in Mary Plummer's eyes. She was gutsy, she had trusted him, they had got on well during the past weeks, and he found her disillusionment almost intolerable.

At that moment the pallid fox suffered the greatest mental strain since the attack on his wife and her death. Harper's investigations into the crime seemed to be getting nowhere; according to Bill Owen, Harper was 'still frigging about looking for a psycho with a hair fetish'.

Suddenly Harry King made up his mind.

'Mary,' he began, and swallowed.

'What?'

'Nothing much.'

He thought he could trust her. But she in turn trusted Alice Caldwell. An unwise word or two, even an innuendo in defence of him to Alice, and it would all get back to Dicker. Dicker was no slouch. Like many fat men with small eyes, he was probably as suspicious as a wild animal. Harry King hoped he was. So Harry pulled his upper lip and said no more.

'You saw Dicker last night,' he heard her say. 'And you got beaten up afterwards. And the house wrecked.'

'Not me. I didn't get hurt. Other people did. And I turned Dicker down. I was going to tell you about it.'

She looked at him, head characteristically on one side, like a thrush listening for another worm.

'I hope so, Harry, I hope so. We've got to trust each other, you know; yes, we have. Otherwise it's *no go*, is it?'

He saw the meaning behind the words, and the meaning was, 'Otherwise *you go* – and *I stay*.'

'Look, I turned Dicker down, didn't I? I never promised him a thing – or a penny.'

'I should hope not. It'd have been the end of a short and beautiful friendship. Ours.'

'All I've been thinking is, was I wise to turn him down flat? Kind of cut him off short. Maybe I should have played along a bit, learnt a few more details of what he has to offer. Kept the options open. Is it wise to chop a talk off quickly?'

'Yes, it is. It wouldn't have got you anywhere. The buck stops here, Harry.'

III

Her foot had stopped waving up and down, her fingers were no longer tapping the side of the chair. She'd keyed herself up for the show-down. Now she'd made her point, loud and clear, and she could relax.

She said again: 'The buck stops here, Harry. Like Truman said, or somebody.'

But this time she spoke in a soft and more friendly tone. King whistled briefly, a long-drawn-out single note, like some bird in a hedgerow. An iron butterfly. He'd suspected it. Now he knew it, and felt admiration. He didn't care for iron butterflies, but this one had gold mixed in somewhere. The alloy was attractive – not all hard, not all soft.

'You can depend on me not to do anything to prejudice your interests, Mary.'

'Or your own,' she said, but softened the words with a smile, and went back to her room. He again had to repress a pang of regret for his deception.

She would have to look after herself. He had to be secretive with her, and cunning with gabby Alice Caldwell.

He again faced the fact that what he planned was murder. With malice aforethought.

CHAPTER EIGHT

Mr Alf Bauer, of Bauer & Bauer & Co., solicitors, considered that he had a difficult role to play in life. He was one of a small band of lawyers who specialised in making sure that his criminal clients, and he had no doubt that most of them were guilty of the offences with which they were charged, had a fair crack of the whip in Court. In fact, so far as he could, he ensured that they had more than a fair crack. He also made sure that he himself had a reasonable share – some said more than reasonable share – of such money as was available for legal fees from his clients. There was, in addition, a small rake-off, undeclared to the tax authorities, from some of the barristers whom he selected to defend his clients in Court.

The precise amount of the rake-off was never discussed. It was left to the discretion and generosity of the barristers concerned, and was paid in cash, in an envelope, when the case was over, and whatever the result. But though the amount was never specified or discussed, it became known on the legal grape-vine that the less generous barristers – mean-minded bastards, Mr Bauer called them, if pressed, and often did, even when not pressed – did not figure often among those who appeared in Court on behalf of Mr Bauer's clients.

At the same time – and here lay the difficulty, and in some measure his danger – Mr Bauer was well aware that it was to his advantage, risky though it was to limb, and even to life, to keep on good terms with the police as far as normal prudence allowed. In the process of what he called 'playing the system' Mr Bauer was often able to glean the strength of a case against a client: whether he should go all out for an acquittal, or save powder and shot and plump for mitigation and a lenient sentence. Most of his clients naturally pressed for a spirited declaration of innocence. But he no more believed his clients than he had believed his wife when, in their courtship days, she had vehemently denied a charge of shop-lifting.

Mr Bauer affected a Dickensian air. His little office off the Strand, London, was impressively lined with legal tomes which he rarely consulted. He himself wore pinstriped trousers, a black jacket, a stiff wide-winged collar, and a big knotted tie. He carried a silver snuff-box, and offered it to clients. (But although there were appropriate traces of snuff on his coat, and he went through the motions of using it, he never actually did so because it made him sneeze.) His shirt cuffs and collar were never quite white at the edges, though it was said in the underworld that he always put on a clean shirt for the Queen's Birthday.

His secret association with the police was of use to Mr Bauer and had helped him gain a not inconsiderable reputation in the criminal world as an astute operator in the war between crooks and the police. He was known to them as an All Right bloke on the whole and one who never showed the slightest disapproval of what his clients had done – a form of bland comfort which was soothing. As an example, it was said that if somebody assaulted a blind matchseller and robbed him of the money in his tray, Mr Bauer would indignantly point out that it was the beggar's fault for so thoughtlessly flaunting his wealth. He was also very plausible. As one thug remarked: 'We all know that most of us would put a foot in the upturned face of a swimming comrade in order to scramble on to a crowded raft, but Alf Bauer's the only bloke who could prove that this was actually in the interests of the drowning man because a less crowded raft might soon come along and pick him up.'

There was, of course, a certain amount of give and take between Mr Bauer and the police, who did not meet him because they liked the yellowish colour of his small eyes, or the cut of his sparse grey hair. And if from time to time some small timer was chopped and sent to prison, that was only to be expected. The big timers did not mind, or enquire into the tragedy too deeply, even if they had vague suspicions that some hint had somehow been wafted on the wind and picked up by the Met. Indeed, there were always one or two cynics who thought that the hint wafting might have been started by a big timer to dispose of a rival who was becoming too big for his boots.

Chief Superintendent Harper regarded Mr Bauer, lawyer and casual informant, as his personal possession. He briefed and debriefed him himself in a back room of a public house on the outskirts of Reigate, run by a retired naval petty officer who had a friendly and helpful nature where the police were concerned. Now, over a starter, a pint of ale, in the same back room, the Superintendent wasted no time in small talk but came straight to the point.

'About Buller, Mr Bauer. Where is he?'

The Superintendent was not on Christian-name terms with Bauer. He reckoned that formality lent a certain dignity to the dusty little man which he did not otherwise possess, and to a relationship which was necessarily furtive.

'Mr Buller?'

'Yes, Buller. Maybe I didn't speak clearly.'

Mr Bauer opened his snuff box and took a pinch of snuff between his first finger and thumb; after an elaborate flourish of his hand, during which he satisfactorily scattered the powder into the air, he applied the finger and thumb to his right nostril and, with a contented look, deeply sniffed up nothing at all. The operation was completed by touching his nose with a red handkerchief. It was what the acting profession call stage 'business', and had the advantage of giving him time to collect his sharp wits and to think.

'Am I my brother's keeper, or rather my client's keeper, Mr Harper?' he asked.

Harper, who had been staring at a picture of some old-time barefisted boxers squaring up to each other, swung his long rectangular head round and pointed his big high-bridged nose at Bauer.

'Look, we don't want any boxing and coxing, do we? Harry King's wife – '

Mr Bauer nodded quickly. 'I know, I know, I read

of the assault in the papers. A most unfortunate business, but my client Mr Buller – '

'It's more unfortunate now. Mrs King died the day after.'

'Died?'

'So it's going to be a murder rap. See what I mean?'

Mr Bauer scratched his scalp, then looked down at his hands and began to clean his right-hand finger-nails with a nail on his left hand. 'I'm sorry. That's terrible.'

'Yes, it is. The buzz tells me that Mr King's in a mean mood. So am I, come to that. Men in a mean mood do mean things if they don't get what they want. Mr King's no longer in the Met. He's what you might call a freelance. I can't control his actions.'

Mr Bauer licked his lips. 'Does he know – about you and me?'

'Not yet,' Harper said.

'Meaning?'

'Meaning what I say – not yet. I want to talk to Buller – where is he? Withholding information, obstructing the police, being an accessory after the fact – '

'You don't need to teach me the law.'

'Nor how to bend it.'

'That's not friendly.'

'I haven't got a friendly disposition.'

Mr Bauer sighed and said:

'Sometimes I don't know why I play along with you, Mr Harper.'

'I do. Because you have to. Goes back twenty years, doesn't it? You were glad of a dab in the fist in those days. Not that I'd shop you to the villains, Mr Bauer.

I wouldn't shop you to your clients. It wouldn't be ethical,' he added. 'But Mr King might. If I told him. I haven't yet, have I? You wouldn't be here if I had. You'd be in hospital – or a morgue. It's not only small-timers you've helped to get sent down.'

Mr Bauer was shocked. Hitherto, there had always been sweetness and light, a civilised exchange of information over a pint or two of beer. Now this.

'Come, now, Mr Harper, aren't we jumping to conclusions? *You* were at Mr Buller's trial a year or two ago.'

'Yes, I was. He must have been grateful to you, Mr Bauer, for helping him to get such a light sentence.'

'Oh, he was, he was!'

'You heard the threat he made from the dock when he was sentenced, "I'll get you, copper, I'll get you where it hurts most, and then I'll get *you*." Somebody has got at Harry King where it hurts most – got his wife.'

Alfred Bauer spread his hands in a despairing gesture, waving them to and fro, and raised his small, watery eyes, and shook his head.

'It was most ill advised of Mr Buller to speak like that, Mr Harper, most ill advised!' He lowered his voice, and leaned forward as though about to confide a private secret. 'But you know what they are, at that level in the – er – that world? It was not the prison sentence which worried him.'

'I should think not.'

'As an up and coming man in those circles, it was the humiliation of getting caught, the lowering of his prestige, so to speak, which upset him and prompted that unfortunate outburst. I did not think his words were to be taken seriously.'

'Neither did we,' snapped Harper.

Bauer hastily corrected himself. 'What I meant to say was, I did not and *do* not think he meant his words seriously.'

'He's your client. But don't get too rigid, you got other people to consider.'

'Such as who?'

'Such as you, and your own skin, and such as me, and Mr King, who might want to ask you a few questions himself. If I told Mr King, of course.'

'Now, now, now,' muttered Bauer, 'we don't want to get all het up and hasty, do we?' He laughed shakily.

Harper banged down his beer mug on the table, so loudly that Bauer jumped.

'And we don't want to get too bloody cheeky, do we? Not when we're in no position to be. You ever seen anybody who's been slashed and bashed by villains, Mr Bauer?'

Bauer ignored the question.

Harper pressed him further: 'You ever seen anybody who's been roughed up by the lads, gone over by the boys – some lads, some boys! – eh? Face slashed, ribs stove in, bloody mouth with teeth gone, crutch a swollen mess. Nice job you'd be for Mrs Bauer to nurse back to health. If she could. If she wanted to.'

Bauer licked his lips, head lowered, weak eyes staring across the room, peering past Harper; not looking at him.

'You don't want to lose me, not after all these years. I'm useful to you, Mr Harper. I've given you good stuff. What about Dick Turner and his mob, and the Scottish bank job? Have you forgotten that one, Mr Harper?'

'Dick's due out, soon,' Harper said. 'Dick wouldn't forget *you*, either – if he knew.'

'Knew what?' Bauer said in his soft, yet grating voice. 'It'd be bad for recruiting if I got hurt, wouldn't it?'

'Recruiting?'

'Recruiting people like me. Outside helpers, so to speak.'

'You mean informers, narks?' Harper said brutally. He got up and walked once round the room and sat down again. 'Know what?'

'Know what?' asked Bauer uneasily.

'I'd rather be a copper without a single good working informant than I'd be you.' He pulled himself up abruptly. Harper could be obscene if necessary. He didn't think it was needed now. Bauer was toying with a cigarette between nicotine-stained fingers. When he put the cigarette to his mouth it quivered. But he had a last fling.

'So it's quits, isn't it? Fifty-fifty?'

Harper scratched his upcurving chin with the sensual dewlap.

'Maybe,' he conceded, 'maybe at your age it is, if you ignore the stove-in ribs and missing teeth. Maybe, yes. Maybe it might even be a relief to Mrs Bauer, in some ways,' he added nastily. 'At your age, I mean.'

He got up again, and forced himself to let a hand drop in friendly fashion on Bauer's shoulder, instinctively, remembering his advice to young officers: fight with a contact if you must, but always part on friendly terms if you want to keep him. He wanted to keep Bauer, though he guessed he didn't like the man any more than Bauer liked him. They were locked in an uneasy association. He always wanted information, and Bauer always wanted money, and silence about being a nark.

He had a final shot to fire at Bauer.

'Short one for the road, Alf?'

Bauer looked up. It was the first time the Superintendent had called him by his Christian name.

'Thank you. Scotch, please. I bear no grudge, when there is plain speaking on both sides,' he said carefully. He would have liked to call the Superintendent by his Christian name in return, but had forgotten it if he had ever known it.

Harper got up to fetch the drinks, leaving an envelope behind which he casually pushed in Bauer's direction. Bauer pocketed it with an air of assumed indifference. It wasn't much but, like other small perks, it all mounted up, and many a mickle made a tax-free muckle.

When Harper returned with the drinks, they formally raised their glasses and drank each other's health like the old pals they weren't.

'There's one last thing,' Harper said, putting down his glass. Bauer's heart sank. The Christian name and the Scotch and the hand on the shoulder had been softeners. Now the sting was coming. Yet when it came he was surprised at first – and then not surprised.

'Listen carefully. I need to know Buller's whereabouts.'

'So I have gathered.'

'Urgently.'

Bauer nodded, finished his whisky at a gulp. 'So as to arrest him on a charge of murder. You put me in a difficult position, Mr Harper.'

'You've been in a difficult position for twenty years.'

'It's worse now.'

'Yes, it is.'

Bauer sighed. It was back to square one. He said mournfully:

'If my client Mr Buller is arrested, charged with murder, found guilty, I shall lose him for a number of years. He is a man of some influence – in certain circles not without money. He would be, as it were, out of circulation for some time.'

'If he's not arrested you'll lose him for good. Let me tell you the fact of life, Alf.'

Bauer pricked up his ears. It was 'Alf' again now. Better, but one had to be careful.

'If there is anything you think I should know as Mr Buller's legal adviser,' Bauer began carefully, stopped, and went off on a different track. 'I am like a juggler, juggling with three Indian clubs – my duty to my client, my duty to the police as a citizen, and my duty to – my own skin, as you would put it.'

Harper nodded. 'Your duty to your client is simple. Let him be arrested and charged. I warn you, and you can pass on the warning: Fred Buller's safer in prison than out of it.'

Bauer smiled superciliously.

'Mr Harper, I am too old a hare to be tempted by

that lettuce leaf – words attributed to the emperor Justinian by Mr Robert Graves; the author, you know.' He took another pinch of snuff, but this time did not properly disperse the dust and he sneezed. 'So is Mr Buller, my client. Far too old a hare,' he said when he had dabbed his nose with his red handkerchief. 'Anyway, there's no case against my client, and, if I may say so, you know it.'

Harper tossed his head impatiently, and began to tick off points on his fingers. 'One – he's known to have made threats against King. Two – he has been seen in King's neighbourhood, looking at King's house. Three – it was a job by an expert criminal: no fingerprints, no clues. Four – Mrs King, Laura King, only spoke about a dozen words before she finally died: "stocking over head" – a criminal habit; "Very strong" – and to her husband "no revenge, darling, too dangerous." By implication – '

'Implications cut no ice in Court, especially those of a dying woman. I could drive a cart and horse through your case – if you had one.'

'Then give me a tip off about where he is. Let me turn Buller in, in his own interests.' Superintendent Harper watched Bauer twisting his nicotine-stained fingers round each other. Bauer looked up and said:

'Whose side are you on, anyway? My client's? Mr Buller's?'

'I'm on the side of the law,' Harper said, and tried to offset the pompous cliché by adding: 'I'm paid to be, aren't I? I don't want Buller killed by Harry King, do I? But he will be, unless – '

'He wouldn't dare,' muttered Alf Bauer. 'Motive too

obvious. Sorry, Mr Harper. Even if I could help you, divided loyalties – ' he spread his hands with a hopeless gesture.

'Your only loyalty is to yourself, Alf Bauer. I repeat that it's in the interests of your client, and of yourself – '

'And I repeat, Mr Harper, that I am too old a hare, and so is Mr Buller, to be tempted by that lettuce leaf – '

Harper got up and moved round and sat on the edge of the table which had separated them, his legs dangling.

'Yes, you're an old hare, and Buller's a hare too,' he said softly. 'Both old hares. But I'll tell you something. King is stalking one old hare. Right now, at this moment. He's got friends from his old days in the Met. He's got sources, like I have. Like I have *you*,' he added with an expression which could be interpreted as either a smile or a sneer. 'He's after Buller. Slowly, plod, plod, plod. Tell that to your client. Tell him to watch out when he hears footsteps behind him at night. Or a noise in the house in the early hours. Not that it'll do him any good. He'll get him in the end. He'll kill him. I don't know how. But I wouldn't like to be killed by Harry King in his present mood. No, I wouldn't. Then he'll merge into his undergrowth again, lead a normal life, 'cos his mind will be as much at rest as it ever can be. He'll have thrown Buller's blackened soul at Laura's feet. The grey fox's revenge. But unlike a fox killing there won't be a pile of feathers left behind. Only Buller's body. Are you listening?'

Bauer nodded. 'I'm listening,' he whispered.

'Good, 'cos I'm telling you he'll then come after *you*, if he learns you obstructed law and order. He's very keen on law and order, is Harry, except now and then. You still listening?'

'Yes, 'course I am.'

'So it's a race, isn't it? Between Harry and me. Either I get Buller for questioning, or Harry gets him.'

Harper lowered himself from the table, edged along the seat on which they were now sitting, pushed his beer mug carefully to the centre of the table, and extended his left arm along the back of the seat.

'Alf?'

'What?'

'You're boxing and coxing. I know you are. I've got proof you are, Alf. I don't care for it, Alf. Not one bit, Alf. Harry King wouldn't care for it, either. You're lucky he isn't here, Alf. But I am.'

Suddenly, he jerked his left arm forward and grabbed the back of Bauer's jacket and shirt. His grip tightened as he turned the knuckles of his hand inwards, towards Bauer's neck.

Bauer began to gasp, and raised his left arm, and clawed at Harper's wrist, struggling and sucking in air. Harper leaned forward and swung his right arm in front of Bauer, and knocked Bauer's left forearm down, so that the wrist struck the table and the glass of his wristwatch splintered; as Bauer twisted his wrist a fragment of glass lightly scratched him.

'Are you going to stop being shifty?' asked Harper coldly.

'Not being shifty. I don't know – '

Harper dragged him to his feet and away from the

table, pushed him to the centre of the room, and forced him to his knees.

'Are you going to stop shilly-shallying?'

'Judges Rules!' muttered Bauer. 'Judges Rules!'

Harper made a sound between a snort and a laugh, and bent his knees and lowered himself so that his knees were resting on Bauer's shoulder blades. He bent down until his great nose and up curving chin were within a few inches of Bauer's right ear.

'Judges Rules, Alf? You're not under arrest, you're not charged with anything. Forget 'em!'

He got to his feet and began to push Bauer around the room, occasionally forcing him to his knees and bouncing him up and down.

'Are you going to stop boxing and coxing, Alf?'

It was Alf all the time now. Like good friends.

'There's nothing I can tell you!'

'Let's take another run at it,' Harper said, and began the pushing and bouncing again. No bones to be broken, no noticeable bruises. No injuries except a slight scratch on one wrist. Just jostling and discomfort and humiliation and no idea of how long it would go on. After three or four minutes, they heard a noise at the door of the room. Harper looked round and frowned. Bauer got to his feet and began to dust himself down, and looked at Nicholls, the landlord, standing in the doorway with empty beer mugs in each hand.

'This is a police officer,' Bauer said shakily. 'I intend to lodge a complaint against him with the Commissioner of Police.' Wounded pride was making him reckless. 'You saw what happened?'

Nicholls nodded.

'The gentleman was calm and composed throughout the interview, sir.' He paused, watching Bauer lick the small scratch on his wrist and examine his broken watchglass. 'Except for one brief moment that is, when he aimed what seemed to be a vicious blow at you, with his mug, which you were fortunately able to ward off with your own mug. As a result the gentleman suffered a slight scratch and damage to his watch. Otherwise, he was calm and composed.'

'I thought he was,' Harper agreed solemnly. 'Bring us a couple more Scotches, Nick, there's a good lad.'

Back to the old formula. Whatever the quarrel, always try to part on good terms with your informant. He and Bauer had a love–hate relationship. Neither wished permanently to estrange the other. But the balance of power was weighted on Harper's side; he knew it, and Bauer knew it. Harper had only to blow him and he'd be chopped by the villains.

Most ordinary citizens, inexperienced in such affairs, would have believed Bauer when he had denied knowing anything helpful about Buller. Harper could not have explained why he knew that Bauer had been boxing and coxing, as he called it.

'Let's start again,' he said, as he gently forced Bauer down on to a chair.

'From where?' Bauer asked apprehensively.

'From where we left off.'

Bauer sighed. 'All right. But there's not much,' he added quickly.

'Let's have what there is.'

'I have reason to believe that my client, Mr Buller, is currently in Amsterdam, Holland, and that he left for

Amsterdam shortly after – the morning after Mrs King was so unfortunately – ' he paused.

'Murdered,' said Harper succinctly.

'Shall we say, more accurately – after she had received injuries from which she subsequently died?'

'Slice it how you like, but go on. How do you know?'

Alf Bauer sighed again. This was the tricky part, and he guessed what Harper's reactions would be. 'An envelope was conveyed to me on the day of Mr Buller's departure. Or I should say conveyed to my office,' he added in his pedantic way.

'I know; go on,' Harper said brusquely. 'That's why I've been asking you – '

'Asking!' muttered Bauer, and flicked his eyes at Harper. 'Have you been keeping my office under observation?' he asked indignantly.

'Your office is one of several in the building,' Harper replied smoothly. 'We keep many offices under observation, for many reasons. Sometimes in the interests of the tenants. What was in it?'

'A letter from Mr Ernest Dicker. Asking me to accept for safe-keeping an enclosed sealed envelope. You will know that Mr Dicker, also a client of mine, is a partner with Mr Buller in the running of a perfectly reputable marriage agency.'

Harper nodded, said sarcastically: 'You didn't steam open the envelope, of course?'

'I considered it prudent discreetly to ascertain the contents. In my business, one has to be prudent.'

'Go on being prudent.'

'Certain documents were in it. For use perhaps in some emergency.'

Bauer paused and looked at Harper scornfully.

'You're not going to be able to pin Laura King's death on my client. There were three signed statements. Two from cousins of my client, with whom I've had dealings, and one from a friend of his whom I have also helped – professionally, of course – legally. They stated that Mr Buller was at a social gathering with them – I forget the address – at the material time.'

'Dates?' asked Superintendent Harper bleakly.

'The statements were undated. Just, "At the time of the offence I hereby swear – " – or "On the evening of the crime in question, Mr Buller was – " that sort of thing. Good enough alibis to raise doubts in the mind of a jury, Mr Harper.'

'Typed statements?' asked Harper.

'Yes,' said Bauer reluctantly.

'Just needing a date typed in by the same typewriter?'

Bauer nodded uneasily. 'Open blank cheques. Evidence of premeditation,' Harper said shortly. 'Valuable evidence of premeditation.'

'Circumstantial evidence. Mere speculation! You know you wouldn't get any mileage out of it,' Bauer sneered.

'Let me have the statements.'

Bauer shook his head. 'Look,' he said quietly, 'what's the use? It's no good pushing those boys around like you did me. No good, no way. They come of a very old criminal family, Mr Harper.' He spoke with respect, much as in other circles reference might be made to a very old County Family. 'They got tradition, see? Reputation. Experience.'

'Whose side are *you* on?' asked Harper, aggressively.

'Me? I'm on everybody's side.'

Nicholls brought in the second tot of whisky.

'Your good health,' Bauer said without much enthusiasm, raising his glass.

'And yours,' Harper said grimly. 'I hope it lasts.'

Neither of them spoke for a few seconds. Then Superintendent Harper said suddenly, 'Hairdresser's assistant, that was Buller's first job in life, wasn't it?'

Bauer nodded indifferently. 'He was really interested in it, too. But it was his downfall. A gentleman will sometimes take his jacket off before he sits in the chair. And leave his wallet in it. I'm afraid young Mr Buller got nicked after the third wallet. But he'd acquired a taste for what some term easy money. Pity.'

Harper sat staring at the picture of the old-time pugilists on the opposite wall. He said: 'His last prison report said he had worked industriously and even with some talent – not that there was much opportunity for talent in the prison barber's shop. Often pleaded to be allowed to work longer hours than normal. Experimented with trying to make wigs. Is he wearing a wig in Amsterdam?'

'Why should he be? Mr Dicker said in his covering letter to me that Mr Buller was going to Amsterdam on marriage agency business, to do with setting up a new branch in Holland. And on other business.

'Mr Dicker telephoned this morning,' Bauer added. 'He wishes for Mr Buller's envelope back. I sent it. By hand.'

'When?'

'About noon.' He paused.

'My client, Mr Buller, will be returning soon.' Bauer blurted out the words.

'I know.'

'How did you know?'

'That's my business.'

'If you knew so much, why the—?' He gestured hopelessly at the room and floor where Harper had bounced him around.

'I wanted corroboration of the Amsterdam information. And something else – I didn't know what was in the envelope, did I?' Harper said. 'It figures. Fixing an alibi in advance. Mind you, I guessed he would have done.'

He massaged his big beak of a nose, then suddenly said: 'Hair.'

'What about hair?' Bauer was puzzled.

'I'd forgotten about your client's early crimes. We weren't all that interested in those. You know what a fetish is? You must.'

Bauer nooded. 'I have not come across one myself, but I would say, at a hazard, that fetishes are concerned with – what, how shall I describe it?'

'Have a go.'

Bauer peered at Harper with his watery eyes.

'Well, I would say an individual with a fetish has an exaggerated, unnatural – er, unhealthy – obsession with some particular substance or thing. Like leather. Or rubber. Or bicycle saddles, or – '

'Or hair,' Harper prompted.

'Hair?'

'Hair. Well, you may or may not recall that the unfortunate Mrs King's assailant hacked off much of her hair. I'm not suggesting that was the real reason for the attack. Far from it. But it was an unexpected bonus, shall we say? One which the assailant found it impossible to resist.' Harper nodded in agreement with himself. 'That makes another point against your client.'

Bauer shook his head. 'I feel that Mr Buller is now more interested in other things.'

'I only hope,' said Harper, 'that your client Buller doesn't try to slip back into this country clandestinely, wearing one of his own wigs. If he does I hope our port people pick him up on my behalf. I hope I get him before Harry King does. For his sake.'

'I don't think Mr King would dare – Mr King has a regard for his own skin. He's only human.'

'Wrong,' snapped Superintendent Harper. 'Harry used to be human. He's not now. He's a fox. A grey fox. A heartless fox.'

He got up. 'Let me know anything you hear. Ring me at home. Call yourself – what? – call yourself Hare, Mr Hare. Say you've got a better lettuce leaf than before.'

They went out of the pub by different doors.

Superintendent Harper was at one with Harry King. Both wanted to get Buller. Harper had an organisation behind him, but had to work within the cold strait-jacket of regulations. Furthermore his approach was different from that of Harry King; so were his interrogations. Harry would have got nothing out of Bauer. Harper had got little that he didn't know, but it was something. Striving to save Harry King from himself, knowing that Harry would kill Buller if he got at him first, knowing he himself would in the end arrest Harry, he used, ironically, methods which Harry would not have approved in order to put Buller safely behind bars.

Apart from minor differences about methods of interrogation, Harper was an orthodox police officer. Rules were rules (on the whole), and the Law was the Law, and if he had to arrest his old colleague Harry King it couldn't be helped.

As he drove away from the pub near Reigate, he told himself that it was only a question of time. Buller might slip into Britain unnoticed. Harper accepted that, and he would put a watch on Buller's flat and on Ernest Dicker and the office of the Round Circle marriage agency. He would get him in the end.

But in what condition? Alive or dead? He had no illusions about Harry King. Harry was an ex-police officer. More than that. Harry was cunning and experienced. If he planned to kill Buller and get away with it, he might just succeed.

As he approached London, Superintendent Harper tried further to sort out his thoughts and feelings. They were confused. Far more confused than Bauer realised. Harper hoped that his superiors at the Yard did not know what was going on in his mind. Otherwise they might muck things up – with the best of intentions, of course. Strait-laced and straightforward, that was their trouble. Even more than he was.

He pulled the car into the side of the road to light his pipe, to distil his medley of thoughts down to essentials and anchor them to firm bases.

Anchor 1: He agreed with King that Buller had killed Laura King. For what reason or reasons did not matter. He had killed her.

Anchor 2: Harry King was going to kill Buller, unless Buller were arrested first.

Anchor 3: If that happened, Harper would go through the usual murder routines.

But he didn't want Buller killed. He didn't even want to arrest Buller – yet. Not after his visit to Amsterdam. Buller would be unimportant dead. Buller alive was very important.

Harper thought of his rough dance with Bauer. He hoped and believed that the pressure he had put on Bauer would leak back to Dicker. And thence to Buller when Buller collected his alibi statements.

Anchor 4: Buller was the lead-in to Ernest Dicker. Dicker – Amsterdam – drugs? Dicker was a big fish. Therefore Buller, killer of Laura King, had to be preserved. That was the ironic essential. Some people don't know how lucky they are, thought Harper.

Harry King now had such an obsession about Buller, according to Bill Owen, that Owen feared he would do 'something silly' if and when he could find Buller. 'All today he's been on to me asking about progress in the case. I told him Buller had left the country for Holland and there's nothing the Dutch police can legitimately hold him on,' Owen had said.

Confiding in Harry was not on. No good telling Harry to lay off Buller. Harry had his obsession.

Harper's pipe was drawing well; he thought about pulling out of the layby. But there was a tingling of excitement in his veins. There had been ever since he had learned that Buller had gone to Amsterdam, the trip openly planned. He sat on, watching the traffic flow past.

Was this the breakthrough he had hoped for, planned for – alone, because it was so delicate and lives might be at risk? It was a terrible responsibility. The operation was potentially so vast that the killing of poor little Laura King seemed small by comparison.

Heroin kills in three years, usually via the liver. How many people, especially young people, were Dicker and Buller prepared to kill? Not only in London, in Britain, but all over the world?

He believed what Harry King had told Bill Owen, that there was a marriage agency war on. But it wasn't for the reason Harry thought, which was purely commercial, however unsavoury the source of funds. No: an international network of marriage bureaux under Dicker's control – and he had no doubt that Dicker would be head man, rather than blustering loud-mouthed Buller – would not only be a good and inno-cent investment for their drug riches. It would also, and primarily, be a vast pool, in which swam unhappy fish. Desperate and disorientated fish; fish craving excitement, and fish leading such lonely lives that they would take any chemical which seemed to bring happi-ness and contact with others. They might even become pushers themselves. There was no end to the possi-bilities.

He switched off his line of speculations, and switched on the car engine.

He would get Laura King's killer in the end – he hoped. But that would have to wait. He had bigger fish to fry. Bigger than sharks. Much bigger.

He eased his way out of the layby, thinking of his meeting with Alf Bauer. He felt sure that a small part of that same, properly edited, would get back to Dicker. That would be good. Anything which apparently indicated Harper's main interest still to be Laura King's murder would be welcome to Ernie Dicker, and anything which lulled Dicker into a false sense of security was welcome to Harper. It was not only because of the possible embarrassment involved in arresting a former colleague and friend that Harper was anxious to keep Buller alive.

CHAPTER NINE

A month went by and there was no more news of Buller. Interpol was silent.

Buller was keeping such a low profile in Amsterdam that he seemed to have submerged completely, like a submarine. Whatever business he was supposed to be doing for Dicker was taking a long time. Harry King was uneasy, restless, fearful that Buller might have left the country for good, even gone to South America. He expressed his worry to Bill Owen.

The Chief Inspector shook his head. 'He took his car with him. A ropy, clapped-out old Ford of some kind, not worth shipping to South America. He'll be back, car and all.'

They were having their weekly beer together. Business at the agency was desultory, and there were few names of prospective clients for Owen to pass over the C.R.O. files. King had not mentioned the subject of a paid holiday for Owen and Madge again. Nevertheless Harry King kept in close touch. The meetings were important to him; not least because Harper seemed to be avoiding him when he telephoned with his usual questions about progress. Owen was his main line of communication with the Yard.

'I think Bob Harper's fed up with me,' Harry King said one evening.

Owen did not reply. Then he said casually:

'Bob Harper thinks Buller's having difficulties finding the stuff.'

'What stuff? Did you say stuff or staff? Staff for a Dutch Round Circle branch?'

'Stuff, not staff. Drugs. He thinks the Round Circle organisation is just a cover. We missed out on Dicker in the Buller case. I've been through the file again. There were marginal indications of a connection, but nothing we could pin on him – as you know. He's a big fat slob, but crafty.' Owen took another mouthful of beer and added: 'He'll surface one day, Buller will. Probably bringing his car with him, with the petrol tank stuffed with heroin or something silly. He's not all that bright sometimes. Dicker doesn't think he is either.'

'How does Harper know what Dicker thinks?' Harry King asked sharply.

Owen shrugged. 'I've had an idea over the years that Bob has got an informant in the legal world, on the criminal side. But you know what Bob Harper is. Plays his informants close to the chest. Don't we all?' He smiled and added: 'Buller'll be back one day, that's my opinion. And of course they'll pick him up at the port, him and his car. They can hardly miss him, can they?'

He smiled again and got to his feet.

'It's better that way, Harry. Better for *you*.'

Harry King's heart sank. He was not to know that Owen felt less breezy and confident than he sounded.

Moreover, Superintendent Harper himself was not as

confident as Owen thought him. He had reluctantly come to the conclusion that matters were drifting; in what direction, he could not guess.

But a couple of hours after King had had his discouraging talk with Owen, Harper's phone rang. When he answered it a voice said:

'Mr Hare speaking. I think we should meet. Urgently. Tomorrow. I have a lettuce leaf you'll like to nibble.'

'Same place, same time?'

'Agreed.'

'I hope the leaf is juicy.'

'It is,' said Bauer, and the phone clicked.

Nicholls, the landlord, greeted Harper when he arrived next day, gestured with his thumb towards the private back room, and said, 'He hasn't improved, but he hasn't got any worse.'

Bauer greeted him as though nothing unusual had happened at their last meeting. He needed Harper, or at least Harper's silence, as much as Harper needed his occasional information. Perhaps more so.

He had bought Harper a pint of beer. Harper nodded and picked it up, and said, 'Cheers. Your health. Your *continued* good health.'

Bauer blinked and said pompously:

'I have some information which I trust will make your journey worthwhile.'

'I trust so, too.'

'My client, in whom you are interested – '

'Which one? I have a continuing interest in most of your clients.'

'My client Mr Buller contemplates a visit to this

country in the very near future, Mr Harper, with car. Possibly in two days' time. Heavily suntanned with stuff you can buy in a chemist. Horn-rimmed spectacles. Passport in name of Ronald Hall. All just to avoid inconvenience, Mr Dicker said.'

Harper gave him a heart-warming beam. But Alf Bauer shrank back as though Harper were threatening him with a dagger. Then he took a sip of beer. His face was pale. He wiped some beer from his mouth and tried to formulate some words, but his lips moved noiselessly.

'What's up with you?' Harper asked.

Bauer leaned forward, stared into Harper's eyes and said:

'For God's sake don't do it, Mr Harper! Ernie Dicker wants me to stand by just in case something like that happens, that's why he told me; but that's not the point.'

'What *is* the bloody point? Why are you in such a tizzy?'

'I think only two people know what I've told you, Mr Harper – apart from you. Only two, Mr Harper. Only Ernie Dicker and me know he's coming, and how he'll look. And Ernie's a very suspicious gentleman, Mr Harper. Very. Once or twice when we've been talking I've thought I saw a funny thoughtful look on his face.' The lawyer's voice tailed off.

Harper made an impatient gesture. 'He must know Buller's on the ports' Stop List!'

'Not after all this time, Mr Harper, and not how he'll look. He thinks Mr Buller's in the clear as regards the Laura King murder, especially in view of all those alibis. He thinks you got no case against him and so he's off the List. Neither do I think you've got a case. Technically, of course,' he added hastily. 'He's only here for a day or two, to – to discuss terms with Ernie, about the Dutch – but he's taking precautions – in case of misunderstanding, as you might say.'

'All the more reason to pick him up while we can.'

'Don't do it, Mr Harper, for heaven's sake don't do it!' Bauer implored, panic in his voice. Harper said nothing.

'You didn't need to bounce me around like you did, last time we met here. Treating me like a suspect,' muttered Bauer.

'You *are* a suspect – technically, as you'd put it.'

'I'll let you know where he's staying, if I can,' Bauer wheedled, panic still in his voice. 'If I can, with safety.'

Harper nodded his head, slowly, with seeming reluctance.

'All right,' he said. 'I won't pick him up at the port. You can finish your beer in peace.'

Alfred Bauer looked radiant, like a man who has been reprieved from death.

He had told Harper nothing he did not know already. In view of what he now suspected, Harper had, in fact, already taken Buller's name off the Stop List. He planned to have him tailed, learn more of his movements and contacts in England. It was a risk. They might lose him. But Bauer should be able to help, and would help – if he knew what was good for him. Buller and his car could come in without even a search.

'So you won't have him picked up,' Bauer said,

anxious to confirm the good news. 'Thanks a lot. I'll never forget this.'

'Nor will I,' Harper said.

'I think he'll be staying at the Wargrove Hotel, Bloomsbury. Dicker's moved there to save money. Wargrove Hotel, Bloomsbury,' repeated Bauer.

'I know,' Harper said.

'Sometimes I wonder why we meet, Mr Harper,' Bauer said in a disappointed tone.

'So do I,' said Harper, then relented and added, 'but thanks for the effort.'

They parted soon afterwards, their love–hate relationship unchanged.

Something had gone very wrong in Chief Inspector Bill Owen's life.

Madge had not ceased to rail about his career, and against Harry King. Evenings and weekends were a nightmare now. What was more, Owen could not tell her what was really blocking his promotion. The thought of blokes from A.10 troubled him more and more, especially since he was involved with drugs more than ever. His problems made sure of that – not that purple hearts solved anything permanently. Let alone acid.

Laura's death did not seem to have made any dent in Madge's anger. But worse still, it had not kept his good friend Harry out of danger. On the contrary: it had plunged him deeper into it. Bill Owen's terrible, overwhelming vision, despite all its clarity and its compelling urgency, had changed nothing.

At the point things had now reached, Owen was

faced with a dilemma. Because of Owen's anti-narcotics commitment, Harper had told him about Buller's impending arrival. He did not divulge the source – nor did Owen ask, knowing it would be a waste of breath. The question in Owen's fraying mind was: should he tell Harry King?

His first inclination was totally against it. But perhaps fatigue, on top of everything else, led his thoughts into false channels. At any rate, they suddenly went into reverse.

Alice Caldwell could learn from Dicker of Buller's plans. In a careless moment, she might drop a remark which would alert Harry to them. And Harry might do something silly.

The two men were in the pub together. As the minutes went by, it became increasingly clear to Bill Owen what he should do. He had received a warning. He had done what he could. He had failed. Now he must warn Harry. After the third pint and the final nip of whisky, he suddenly put his hand on King's arm, and said once more:

'Don't do it, Harry. Harper'll get you. Don't do it, boy.'

Harry King stiffened, suddenly alert.

'Don't do what?'

'Kill him. He's coming over in a couple of days. To see Dicker. Harper knows. Don't do it, Harry. Harper'll nick you. Life sentence. Laura wouldn't want it that way.'

His voice was slurred now, but he was happy because he was certain that his mind was crystal clear, had never been clearer, and never would be clearer – no, never. It was as though a beam from a searchlight were illuminating the dangerous path down which his good friend Harry King could walk unless he were given this final, desperate warning and appeal. Owen got unsteadily to his feet. He had fulfilled his mission.

Perhaps the time was coming to make a clean breast of it all. Of everything.

Harry King got up too and took his arm, and said:

'We'll go home together, shall we, Bill?'

He left Bill Owen on his doorstep, his finger pressed on the doorbell, waiting for Madge to open it because he couldn't find his keys.

As he walked the short distance to his own house, Harry King's mind was made up. He knew he had to work fast.

Once in the hall, he peered at the telephone. Finally he picked it up and made an appointment to see Dicker at his hotel at eight o'clock the following evening.

As he hung up, he told himself that he would have to put over the deadliest mixture of lies and bluff in the whole of his life. And that was saying something.

CHAPTER TEN

'I thought you'd be in touch again,' Dicker said when Harry went up to his hotel room.

'You did?'

'Yes, I did. 'Cos you're not a dumb bunny, that's why.'

'A fellow's got to look after himself.'

Ernest Dicker nodded, 'Sure has. If *you* don't, nobody will.'

He had been playing a card game, a form of patience, when King arrived. A bottle of whisky and two empty glasses were on the table, and a third glass, filled with water, which evidently served as a jug. Dicker scooped the cards together and laid them neatly on one side of the table. He slapped his stomach.

'My Ulli, she says, "Viel Holz vor der Tur" – she's German, see? It means "lot of wood in front of the door", like you sometimes find in a German village. It might mean you're doing OK, or maybe just fat.'

Harry King nodded. 'Like we say, "You don't put bay windows in slum property." '

'We do?'

'Sometimes we do.'

'Never heard the expression. I've led a sheltered life.'

'You have? You could have kidded me.'

'Want a slug of whisky?'

'Don't mind if I do.'

'That's what you said last time we met.'

'Still means the same.'

He sniggered and poured out a large helping of whisky into the two glasses, and picked up the tumbler of water. 'How much?'

'About half and half.'

Dicker poured some water into the glasses, and handed one to King. He raised his own glass. 'Good luck. However careful you are, you need it. What's on your mind?'

'About the same as what's been on yours,' said Harry King carefully. 'Silly to fight over the same territory.'

'Hoped you'd see it my way. Thought you would.'

King nodded. Alice Caldwell had done her stuff – tipped Dicker off that her new colleague had a soft centre.

'I've got to look after myself,' King said again. Upright and rigid. Grey and colourless. 'Myself, and maybe you.'

Ernest Dicker put down his glass softly on the table. 'Come again?'

'I said, and maybe you.'

Dicker sighed. 'Want some coffee?'

'Yes, if you do.'

Dicker reached sideways and asked on the house telephone for coffee for three to be sent up.

King raised his eyebrows. 'Three?'

'Somebody else may pop in.'

Harry King's eyes roved around the room. Clinical

white paint everywhere. Bathroom attached, door partly open. Usual bits and pieces: strip of stuff for polishing shoes, needle and cottons, spare buttons and a safety pin. All the normal modern hotel room jazz. Two new-looking suitcases standing against a wall. One with initials, E.D., the other with F.B. Ernest Dicker, Frederick Buller?

'Nice suitcases,' King said politely.

'Yeah,' replied Dicker non-committally. Then he said abruptly: 'What you got to offer?'

'What have *you* got?'

'Peace, like I've suggested before.'

'At a price.'

'Nothing is for nothing.'

'It hasn't been. That's for sure. Not in the past month or so,' King said woodenly, and saw Dicker's eye flicker. For better or for worse, King had put a spark to the trail of gunpowder. There was no turning back now. Something was going to blow up, either in his own face or Buller's. To his surprise he felt calmer than at any time since Laura's death. His mind was cool, even cold: devoid of all emotion, finely tuned to observe, deduce, catch nuances such as the flicker he had seen in Dicker's eyes.

'We can't pay any more,' King said.

Dicker's eyes were like small blue stones. What he was thinking, Harry King hoped, was that if Sure Friendship money had already been paid, for some reason, he, Ernie Dicker, had had no sniff of it.

'Forget the money,' Dicker said unexpectedly. 'For the moment, that is. What else you got to offer?'

'I could lean on Mary Plummer to agree to amalgamation.'

He licked his lips, spoke diffidently, as though he were playing a weak card. Which he was, deliberately. If he judged Ernie Dicker's character right, he must let Ernie do the running and the pressing; King must simulate reluctance and appear to fight desperately for good terms.

'I can lean on her, too,' Dicker said viciously. 'As you know. As you well know.'

Harry King remained silent for a few seconds. Then he said:

'She's tougher than you think.'

'I can be even tougher.'

Dicker went through the motions of thinking, scratched his bald scalp with its fringe of faded blond hair, frowned, pulled his upper lip, sighed and said: 'I could fit Mary Plummer in. To help with the women clients. You can tell her that, if it'll help.'

King nodded. 'And what's in it for me?'

'Plenty. What can you give me?'

'Information.'

'I get plenty of that,' Dicker sneered.

'Not my kind.'

'Such as?'

'The name of a bent copper.'

'Worth having – I suppose,' Dicker said indifferently. He was peeling the wrapping off a cigar and did not look up.

'This one's worth having.'

Dicker took out a small penknife, and opened it,

preparatory to snipping off the end of the cigar. He said:

'Don't give me any crap, will you? Not if you know what's good for you.'

'I know what's good for me,' King said, sitting grey and upright, and tense. 'That's why I'm here, isn't it? I'm not feeding you crap. No lies, no bluff. All on the level.'

He meant it. He had fed Dicker one small lie, implying that Buller had had cash he hadn't passed on. But that was insignificant; a softener. Henceforth it would be true facts. Mostly. Building up to the final push which would end in Buller's death. Even the final push would only involve lies by implication. Suggestions. Mostly unspoken. Leaving Ernie Dicker to draw his own conclusions.

Harry King had no intention of killing Buller himself. He was going to leave that to Dicker.

Meanwhile there would be hard facts. True facts, because he did not propose to underestimate Dicker's grapevine. Dicker would check everything he could – every name, every detail.

King took a sip of whisky and waited for the inevitable question. It came as he was filling his pipe.

'What's his name?'

'Whose?'

'The copper's name.'

King cleared his throat, licked his lips – hesitating, putting on his prepared act of reluctance.

'What's clogging you up?' Dicker asked suspiciously.

'Old instincts,' muttered King sheepishly. 'Old copper instincts – keeping your informant's names to your-self.'

'You're not a copper now. What's his name?'

King gulped, seemed to come to a decision.

'Owen. Bill Owen.'

'Rank?'

'Chief Inspector.'

'Mob?'

'Anti-narcotics.'

'Ah,' said Dicker, and sighed and beamed. He reached for the telephone, asked for a line and dialled a number. When there was an answer: he said:

'Name of Bill Owen mean anything to you? It does to me, of course. Just checking that he's still – still what? *En poste?* What's that, for God's sake? Still in the Force, still doing the same job. That's all I want to know. Thanks, Alf.'

Dicker replaced the receiver.

'My legal adviser,' he said.

Harry King licked his lips again and said casually:

'Owen and Bob Harper are working pretty closely at present.'

'Bob Harper?'

'Superintendent Harper. Serious Crime Squad. They over-lap with the anti-narcotics crowd now and then. When something big's cooking. Like there is now.'

'How do you know?' Dicker asked sharply. 'What gives you that idea?'

'Bill Owen gives me that idea. He got it from Bob Harper, and told me. I see him now and then. He helps check Sure Friendship clients in the C.R.O. We don't want to take on crooks.'

'Oh, dear me, no,' Dicker said, lit his cigar and added harshly:

'How bent is this Owen type, Harry?'

A monitoring voice inside King whispered: softly, softly. Keep a low key. Honest new friend doing his best. Not wanting to claim too much. Keeping to truth. Resist temptation to exaggerate.

'Owen? Well, to be perfectly honest, he's only half bent.'

A faint smile relieved the sombre look on King's face. In the circumstances he enjoyed using the words 'perfectly honest'. But he hoped the smile looked deprecating, half-ashamed, the smile of one who had claimed too much and now regretted it. Dicker took him up aggressively:

'Half bent, is he? I'll bend him good and proper in the end!'

'Not you, Ernie – me. I've got him half hooked.'

He fumbled in a jacket pocket and brought out two return tickets, London–Majorca and back, dated a month ahead, booked for Mr and Mrs W. Owen, and flung them on the table in front of Dicker.

'He needs a rest. He knows it. His wife knows it. If he doesn't get a break he'll crack up. They both know it. He'll take the perks in the end. Then I've got him really hooked.'

'Proper hooked,' agreed Dicker. But he reached for the phone again, and when he had dialled said:

'Alf? Sorry to bother you again, boy. That geezer we were talking about. Any gen on his health? Overwork? Tetchy? Being nagged by his wife? Disappointed professionally? Needs a break? That the buzz? Thanks.'

Harry King had refused a cigar and lit his pipe. Dicker was sniffing the air disapprovingly. 'Filthy smell, that stuff,' he muttered.

King took no notice. He went on puffing, occasionally tamping down the tobacco with his forefinger, feeling the adrenalin building up inside him, preparing him for the final push. When he could bear it no longer he took the plunge, dived in at the deep end, and said:

'Ernie, there's something you ought to know – I think.'

'What's it cost?' Dicker said, but he smiled.

'Nothing. And I'm not accusing anybody.'

'Never said you were.'

'I'm just giving you facts to think about. You won't like what I've got to say, Ernie – and I don't like saying it,' added Harry King, stunned by his own brazenness. 'It's about Fred Buller, Ernie.'

'Go on,' Dicker said uninterestedly.

'People are always talking about bent coppers,' muttered King. 'Coppers aren't the only people who get bent, Ernie.'

Dicker smiled broadly, tolerantly, and said: 'Okay, Harry – you're right to point it out. I guess Fred fiddled me on the protection dough you gave him. That often happens. I'll sort him out sometime. Maybe he just kind of borrowed it. Look, Harry, I know what you think about Fred Buller and the sad death of your dear wife, Harry, but – '

'Why didn't Harper – why didn't the coppers pick him up, Ernie?'

' 'Cos he'd skipped, by luck or as planned, whichever way you look at it – that's why.'

Harry King's face was no longer grey or even pallid. Dicker noted that it was pink, and his eyes were bright and alert. He was in the forefront of the battle now. To win or lose. Dicker was puzzled.

'What's on your mind, Harry?'

'Why didn't they pick him up on his next trip from Amsterdam to here? Or the one after – twice in the last two or three weeks, he's been over. Each time with new suitcases like that one there.'

'Suitcases? How do you know?' asked Dicker loudly, and banged the table so hard that his glass of whisky jumped and nearly toppled over. He picked it up and drained it. 'Come on, Harry, tell me, I need to know.'

'Owen told me. He said he had it from Bob Harper. Harper ought to have pulled him in for questioning about my poor Laura's – '

He stopped. Ernest Dicker didn't seem to be listening. He seemed to be holding his breath, and to have swollen. The skin on his bald head was glistening.

'The port people ought to have held him,' murmured King 'Unless they were told not to – for some reason. He came over quite openly. With a passport in his own name. No disguise, no wig, or dark glasses, or beard or anything like that. They searched the suitcases once. Nothing but ordinary personal belongings. No false bottoms or sides or lids. And nothing in the car.'

'There wouldn't be,' Dicker said.

King relit his pipe.

'I wish you wouldn't smoke that muck, Harry.'

'I'm not smoking it for you, Ernie. They'd go

through the formal routine now and then, wouldn't they – a search, a few polite questions? Sort of cover for him if – '

Dicker shook his head. 'It doesn't make sense, looking at his past – not from where I'm sitting.'

'Looking at his past, it does – from where I'm sitting, Ernie. You know his form. Nicked for swiping wallets when a hairdresser's assistant, nicked for a minor con trick later, but gets off lightly. Suspected of clobbering a white man and a black lad, but not enough evidence against him. No charge. Well, maybe there wasn't. But it adds up.'

'Adds up to what?'

'That's a silly question, Ernie – if I may be so bold. It adds up to what we're thinking – I, and you by now. It adds up to him being sent down for three years for pushing heroin and pot and stuff with a few others but let out on parole after a year. A snout sometimes has to do a short stretch now and then to avert suspicion if he doesn't want to be a dead snout. What are you thinking about?'

'Some of his side-kicks who've gone inside over the years, Harry. Now and then. The boys thought it was bad luck. Me, I had other ideas. Know what I thought? I thought it was old Alf Bauer, the mouthpiece, who'd been grassing – well, I thought it *could* have been. Not that he'd grass on me. I'm worth more to him outside than inside. Now I think I was wrong about Alf,' Dicker said slowly. 'Poor old Alf, I did him an injustice.'

'Buller's coming over again, any time now,' King

said. 'Have a chat with the lad. Be frank and open and – '

He stopped in mid-sentence because Ernie Dicker was staring in front of him with murder in his eyes. 'I know he's coming over. But how do *you* know?'

'From Bill Owen – who had it from Bob Harper.'

'Who had it from who?' asked Dicker, in a low voice.

'Your guess is as good as mine,' Harry King replied, and was about to say something else – but there was a knock on the door, and it opened before Dicker could respond. A room waiter came in carrying the coffee Dicker had ordered. He set it down in front of Dicker. On his way out of the room he paused politely at the door, and Alice Caldwell edged past him and walked in.

Harry King looked at her. 'Well, well,' he said. 'Good evening.'

She looked at him with contempt.

'I thought it would end like this,' she said acidly.

Harry King offered her his chair, but she took no notice. Dicker did not get up. He watched her as she took off her coat and laid it on the bed with her hand-bag. She was wearing a good deal of showy jewellery, which was only right and proper if Ernie had given it to her, King thought. A bloke likes to see his goods on show. She went over and settled herself on Dicker's knees; he put his left arm round her shoulder, tilted her face upwards and started to eat her. She responded eagerly, saying nothing. King felt sick. He thought of a slug eating its way into a young plant. The plant having no objection – seeming to enjoy its own destruction.

After a while Ernie Dicker raised his head, but kept

his arm round her, caressing her shoulder blade. He lowered his head till his second chin sank on to his collar and said:

'You don't want to mind old Harry here, sweetie. He's all right. He's told me a thing or two. He's put me wise to things. I begun to see things clear. And I don't like what I see. No, I don't. Harry's joining us, and he's going to help me do things I like and things I don't like.'

Alice Caldwell straightened herself on Dicker's knees, and glared at King.

'I don't trust him, Ernie,' she said in a voice as soft as her complexion. 'I don't trust him.' It was an open, blatant, insulting challenge, breathtaking in its rudeness.

Harry King could have killed her.

'He's all right, honey bee, he's all right.'

'He's got a soft centre, he'll – '

The telephone rang before she could finish the sentence. Dicker lifted the receiver. King heard a loud voice quacking on the line. Dicker looked at King and winked, and said:

'Why, hello, Fred! Long time no see.'

The voice quacked on.

'Where are you, Fred? Near Dorking? Fred – are you listening? You got another nice new suitcase? You have? Lock needs repairing. Shoddy stuff they make these days, Fred.'

King heard Buller's distant laugh. Then Dicker spoke again.

'Listen, Fred, I got to see you. I got to see you tonight, Fred. It's about the suitcases. It's urgent, Fred.

What? You thick in the head? 'Course I can't tell you on the phone. No, I can't see you in London.'

There was a puzzled noise from the other end.

'Tip-off, Fred,' replied Dicker. Then he winked broadly again at King as he said, 'From Alf Bauer, Fred. He says not to come to London.'

Dicker looked at his gold wristwatch. 'See you at about 2 a.m. Usual place. Bring the suitcase. Park as usual. Walk along the road as usual. We'll be there.' He replaced the receiver.

So far so good, thought King.

But Alice Caldwell was still staring at him, and hostility was still in her eyes. King knew he had to cope with the Alice problem at once. He got to his feet. He said:

'Well, Ernie, I wanted to come in with you, but things being as they are here, I don't think – '

Ernest Dicker interrupted him brusquely: 'Don't take no notice of her, Harry boy. She's a bit of a perfectionist.' He bent down and kissed Alice again and said:

'Listen, honey bee, just keep your pretty trap shut, all right? Harry here knows the score. He's left the Met, he's out on a limb, he's going to lean on Mary Plummer to come in with us, he's got a bent copper as good as in his pocket. He's shown me things about Fred Buller that make me shudder, honey bee, me being honest and loyal, as you know. I'll tell you about them when Fred's gone.'

Alice Caldwell looked round the room, blue eyes wide.

'Gone? Fred's not here.'

'No, and he won't be either. Ever. Fred's a snout,

honey bee. Been grassing for years. Maybe to Harper. Fred Buller's got to go, honey.'

His cigar had gone out. He applied the flame of his lighter to the end, to warm it before relighting it. He guessed that Alice Caldwell was looking at him, bewildered, a trifle apprehensive, and explained himself as one would to a child:

'Listen, honey bee, you know how people talk about taking a dog for walkies?'

Alice Caldwell nodded.

'If it's sick, or they want to have it put down by the vet for some reason they – well, they kind of take it for a long walkies, don't they?'

Alice was staring at him intently. She nodded again. Dicker said:

'Harry King here is going to take Fred Buller for a long walkies, see? Harry doesn't love Fred at all, Harry hates his guts; it'll be a pleasure, won't it, Harry?'

Harry King knew Alice was looking at him speculatively.

'Yes, I hate his guts, I wish him dead, I wish him in hell. It'll be a real pleasure, Ernie. It'll sort of make us – ' He paused groping for words.

'Blood brothers?' suggested Ernie Dicker.

King nodded. 'Blood brothers,' he agreed enthusiastically, 'that's right – blood brothers. But Buller's blood, not ours. What's the plan?'

'Usual. He'll park at Newlands Corner, between Dorking and – oh, Ripley or some damn place – and walk backwards and forwards, shining a torch on the grass verge as though he's lost something. Then I slow down and pick him up with his suitcase, and Bob's your uncle.' Dicker started to maul Alice Caldwell again, and said: 'Next time it's you and me who'll go to Amsterdam for suitcases, honey bee.'

'That'll be the day,' she murmured, eyes shining.

'That'll be the night, you mean,' Dicker said giving one of the sniggering high-pitched laughs which went badly with his great bulky body.

'And tonight?' she asked.

'We meet in the same place, like you heard me tell him. Go through the same drill – except for one thing.'

'What thing?'

King was sitting motionless, nerves taut.

'Except we don't stop, that's what.'

'Just slow down. You got a silencer on your gun, Ernie?' King asked in a low voice.

'Who mentioned a gun, Harry? I said we don't stop – or slow down, come to that. We go faster. Or rather you do. You'll be driving. We'll be in my heavy Rover, and we don't stop, 'cos you ain't familiar with the car, are you, and when you want to stamp on the brake pedal you stamp on the accelerator instead. Too bad.'

'Crash tinkle-tinkle,' Alice Caldwell said softly, her eyes on King's face.

'Hope not. Headlamps cost money. Hope it's just thud-crump-thud,' Dicker said. 'What you might call hit-and-run.'

'What if he's not dead?' Alice Caldwell said, her gaze still fixed on Harry King's face. He was astounded that anyone so pretty and flower-like could discuss murder so unemotionally.

'Then Harry goes into reverse and has another go, don't you, Harry?'

159

King nodded.

'That's my boy! End of a bloody double-crossing snout. Just to encourage the others,' Dicker said, again turning red in the face. 'Bastard, bloody bastard!'

He had been patting Alice Caldwell's knee. He stopped doing so and stared at her. 'I've just thought of another thing, honey bee.'

'What?' Alice switched her gaze from Harry King to Dicker.

'Remember that time we met at the Hilton?'

'Yes.' King thought he detected a trace of alarm in her voice.

Dicker said slowly: 'I remember now – I got a faint idea, wasn't no more than that, about a couple of types hanging around in the room where we were having our coffee.'

Alice Caldwell nodded. 'Me, too.'

'Thought they were a couple of hotel dicks.'

'Me, too,' Alice said again.

'In the light of what our friend has pointed out about other things I've changed my mind, honey. I reckon they were dicks all right – but not hotel dicks. Just ordinary plain-clothes cops, honey. It figures.'

Alice nodded agreement.

So did Harry. But his thoughts were elsewhere.

The explosion had taken place. Buller was doomed. But now there was this blow-back. He didn't know what he had expected Dicker to do exactly. Kill Buller himself? Get a couple of thugs from somewhere? He hadn't thought the detail through. Detail? It was a focal point. He saw that now. Detail indeed! He gave a pallid smile.

'What's the joke?' Dicker asked sharply.

'Just thinking of the look on Buller's face before he's hit.'

But he ceased to smile. Laura had been right when she had pleaded for no revenge. Bill Owen had been right. Harper would get him in the end.

He wondered if it was too late to back down. He had a feeling that, if he did, Dicker and Alice between them would kill Buller and then frame him. As if she had been reading his thoughts, Alice slipped off Dicker's knees, groped under the bed and brought out a little tape recorder.

Dicker pointed at it.

'We've been on the air, so to speak, Harry boy.'

'You didn't need to.'

'Mutual insurance, Harry. Kind of comforting. No offence meant.'

'None taken,' King said equably.

Alice Caldwell looked at her wristwatch. 'Ten-thirty. Pub's shut. Tom'll be waiting.' She got up, put on her coat and took two suitcases from where they had been standing against the bedroom wall.

'Want a hand?' King asked.

She shook her head. 'They're empty now.'

'Has Tom cleared the backlog?' Dicker asked.

'The whole lot.'

Dicker grunted approval. 'Just as well. Fred Buller may bring two. They'll be his last two. I know a Dutch bloke who can take his place.'

King shook his head in exasperation. 'I don't get it. Fill me in. Empty suitcases – '

Alice Caldwell swung round, a suitcase in each hand.

'Don't tell him!' she said loudly. 'He hasn't paid his way in yet. And he's got a soft centre.'

'He'll have paid his entrance fee by two in the morning, honey bee.'

He looked at King and smiled, almost apologetically. 'It'll keep till then. Women are queer about secrets. Closer than men, sometimes.'

Alice wasn't listening, and in a few seconds the door closed behind her. Then Dicker thought of something, struggled out of his chair and went to the door and called after her, 'Remember, bring the heavy Rover, not the Ford.' Then he came back and sat down again.

'Damage to the car? Blood stains?' King asked abruptly.

'I got a bloke who'll fix that, no questions asked.'

'I bet you have. We could be stopped on the way back, though.'

'Not if you drive carefully, not too fast, not too slow. Anyway – got to take a risk. Can't pick it up if you don't put it down, Harry.'

CHAPTER ELEVEN

The words rang in King's ears. 'Can't pick it up if you
don't put it down, Harry.'

Darling Lauralie hadn't understood that. But,
wherever she was, perhaps she understood now that
there could be no peace while Buller lived.

The door opened and Alice Caldwell came in.

'Tom get the suitcases?' Dicker asked.

She nodded.

'Got the Rover?'

'It's at the door, lover boy. You can drop me off on
the way.'

Dicker shook his head. 'You're coming too, honey
bee. Might want a third witness that it was – er – the
pedestrian's fault. Driver lost his head and drove on.
We tried to get him to report the accident, but – '
Dicker stopped, looked at King and said: 'It won't
happen, Harry. Just routine – a fail-safe plan, like we
always have. Okay?'

King nodded. The three of them went out of the
hotel and into the night.

Dicker sat in the front passenger seat, Alice Caldwell behind King. King decided to go on the route he
knew – Kensington, Hammersmith, Roehampton, then
the Guildford road as far as Ripley. Left after Ripley,

and finally the road to Dorking, passing Newlands Corner and, on the left, the Silent Pool, a not very impressive small stretch of water with a path round it. King had at first thought that the attack on Buller might be on that path in one form or another, by Dicker or his heavy squad because the tree-shrouded water might have been a useful place in which to dump the suitably weighted body. But such was not Dicker's plan.

King wished it had been. Shooting was one thing: fast and sure and comparatively clean. Deliberate hit-and-run was different. Thud, crump. And a scream? Reversing back to finish the job? Not succeeding? Forward again. As if reading his thoughts, Dicker opened the car's glove drawer in front of him and took out a heavy spanner.

'You can use this, if you prefer. If he makes difficulties.'

King nodded. 'Maybe I will.'

He heard a sound from the back of the car which sounded like Alice Caldwell sucking her breath quickly. Was even she feeling queasy?

Dicker turned his head. 'You don't need to watch, honey bee.'

There was no response for a few seconds. Then she said:

'I'll watch. Ernie. It's what I'm here for, isn't it?'

They were half-an-hour early by the time they reached Newlands Corner. It was a beautiful moonlit night, and mild for the time of year. They cruised slowly past the beauty spot, its splendid view partly visible even at one thirty in the morning. The sky was star-spangled and no breeze stirred the branches of a group of trees. Under them two or three cars were parked facing the view. Dicker pointed them out and laughed.

'Young fellas snogging and necking on the back seat, like Alice and I did here sometimes. But last time it wasn't warm like tonight.'

'It's always warm when you're around, lover boy. After a bit, anyway.'

Dicker laughed and turned to Harry King. 'Pull in to the left, in about half a mile, and run us off the road, when you can.'

King did so, and switched off the engine.

'Keep the parking lights on, Harry. He'll park about five or six minutes' walk away, on the opposite side of the road, facing us, and flash his headlights a couple of times. I've got yellow discs on the headlamps, like as though I've come from the Continent, and he'll have the same. Then he'll get out and walk towards us, on the right-hand side of the road, and you'll flash a couple of times to show you've seen him. Then, when he's started walking – carrying a suitcase, I hope – you start up and drive to meet him. You'll be driving down-hill. Should get up a good speed. Should be quite a meeting. You'll be pleased.'

'I want to see him dead,' King replied through his teeth. 'But supposing somebody sees him lugging his suitcase along the road, hoofing it uphill, and offers him a lift, Ernie?'

'He won't take it, will he? He's meeting us, isn't he?'

'If he's wise he'll take it.'

'But he won't, and he's not wise,' said Alice from the rear seat. 'He's thick. Like the fuzz.'

'Thick as a short plank,' agreed Dicker.

There was silence for five minutes. Alice had lighted a cigarette. Dicker had his chin on his chest, as though dozing, but King saw that his eyes were open and fixed on the road ahead.

Harry King shifted in the driver's seat, finding a more comfortable position. He hadn't wanted it to happen his way.

At one time he would gladly have killed Buller by the most painful means available. Dimly, however, he realised that hate was like love. There is always a climax of hatred – but then, unless it is fuelled up, the emotion subsides. It does not necessarily die; it lives and glows. But it is tolerable.

He wanted Buller to die – but not by his hand, with Lauralie watching from wherever she was, shaking her head disapprovingly. Yet he was committed; he was at the wheel of the Rover, with the big ruthless Dicker beside him, and behind him Alice Caldwell, as quick and deadly as a leopardess with a cub.

Dicker was her cub. Some cub. He smiled briefly. Then he took out his pocket handkerchief and wiped the palms of his hands.

'Got the wind up, Harry?' asked Dicker.

'No.'

'Just as well. Ah, look, there he is, drawing up. See? He flashed. Flash him back. Twice. Go on.'

Harry King did so, and saw Buller get out of the car and walk up the incline towards them.

'He's got a suitcase,' whispered Alice Caldwell.

'He'd better have,' muttered Dicker, illogically since Buller had no future of any kind. 'Okay, Harry. Switch on.'

King put his handkerchief to his mouth. Dicker glared at him. 'What's up with you? Not chickening out?'

King shook his head. 'No, Ernie. I just feel sick. Must be something I've eaten. I think I'm going to throw up, Ernie.' He opened the driver's door and began to scramble out.

'Come back here!' shouted Dicker, and struggled to get his fat thighs over the gear lever into the driver's seat. King ran round the front of the Rover, got into the passenger seat, slammed the door, and heard the engine come alive and the car move forward. Slowly at first, but with gathering speed. 'You got no guts!' Dicker was shouting.

King kept his eyes fixed on the figure walking uphill towards them. Buller made no attempt to get out of the way. King saw the look of surprise and terror in his black eyes before the car hit him. In the headlamps, the look was very clear.

It was all as King had imagined. Thud and crump, but also a slight judder and jolt; then the tyres gripped the road again.

Dicker stopped the car, switched off, muttered an obscenity and Buller's name, grabbed the heavy spanner and walked quickly back to the oblong lump that lay in the road. King, watching through the driver's mirror, and Alice through the rear window, saw Dicker's right forearm rise and began to descend.

Alice whispered, 'Oh!' King said nothing.

They watched as Dicker picked up the suitcase and walked back to the car. He handed it to Alice, took a yellow duster out of a front locker, wiped the spanner and threw that on the floor near Alice's feet. Harry saw her shrink away from it. Then he watched Dicker walk around to the front of the car and wipe it over with the duster, which he threw into the back.

'There'll still be prints on the spanner,' Harry King said.

'I'll put it and the duster in a bloody bin in London,' Dicker shouted and flung himself into the driver's seat, and started the engine. His face was glistening with sweat, and he was in a towering rage as he let in the clutch. 'You'll have to do a bloody sight better than that in future, Harry. That's for sure.'

'It was something I ate,' King said stubbornly.

From the back of the car Alice Caldwell made a remark in a soft quavering voice.

'What?' Dicker asked loudly. 'What did you say? Speak up, girl!'

'I said I told you Harry had a soft centre, Ernie. I've thought it for a long time.'

Dicker did not reply. His eyes were fixed on the road a quarter of a mile ahead, where two cars were drawn up broadside on. Blue lights were flashing from their roofs, and a figure stood in the roadway flashing a torch to and fro.

'Bloody hell,' muttered Dicker. He swung into the entrance to a field, backed and set off on the road he had come along.

A group of figures were gathered round something on the road which had been Buller. Two, who were in police uniform, glanced up as Dicker approached, but took no further notice.

'That's a bleedin' bit of luck,' Dicker muttered, and

Harry heard a deep sigh as Dicker let the air out of his lungs.

At Newlands Corner King noted that people were no longer sitting in cars under the trees, admiring the view in the moonlight, and round the next bend he saw why. Two more cars were drawn up a few yards apart, headlamps blazing, positioned to form another hasty barrier, and again torches were flashing to and fro.

Dicker accelerated. King thought he was going to try to crash his way through. Alice said urgently: 'Don't try it. There's a fuzz car on your tail – he'll overtake in the end, Ernie!'

Dicker hesitated, lost speed, slowed down, and stopped.

'Sod it!' he snarled. 'More bloody grassing.'

'This is it, lover man,' Alice Caldwell said in a hard voice. 'Thanks for the ride.'

A face under a cap with a checkered band peered in at Dicker, signalled him to open the window, and said, 'Excuse me, sir, may I see your driving licence?'

Dicker produced it. While the officer was examining it, another was strolling round the car flashing his torch, bending down from time to time. He joined the first policeman and said:

'Would you please get out of the car, sir? And blow in this bag, sir.'

He did so. The two officers looked at the bag. One said: 'You are Mr Dicker, according to your licence, which seems to be in order.'

'I am.'

'I have reason to believe that your blood stream contains alcohol above the permitted limit for a driver. I must ask you to accompany me to a police station to investigate the matter further.'

'You lead the way, I'll follow,' Dicker said airily.

'No, sir. One of our officers will follow with your car. I have reason to believe it may have been involved in an accident recently. It will be necessary to examine it in its present condition.'

Dicker shrugged. Before walking away with the officer, he turned and waved to Alice Caldwell. 'Be seeing you, honey bee.'

'Not for a long time,' she replied in an unexpectedly metallic voice.

The second officer put his head in the car and said to King: 'It would be helpful if you would accompany us in another car, sir. It's possible we may ask you to make a statement.' He paused and looked at Alice Caldwell. 'And you, madam.'

'May I bring my suitcase?'

'If you wish, madam.'

'I do wish,' Alice Caldwell said firmly.

'So do I,' a voice from the darkness on the other side of the car said jokily. King heard the crunch of feet on the gravelly road as Superintendent Harper approached.

'They can travel in my car,' Harper said.

'Very good, sir.'

In the car, Harper said nothing for a while. When he had put a light to his pipe he said:

'I was afraid you were going to be driving, Harry. Almost sure of it. I'm glad you weren't. It would have been awkward.'

CHAPTER TWELVE

It was some time later when Harry King, sitting in the Sure Friendship office, had an unexpected telephone call from Superintendent Harper.

'I've got some news for you,' Harper said. 'Can you be in my office in an hour?'

Puzzled, King agreed.

He arrived and sat down. Straight away Harper said, 'I'm sorry about this, Harry. Bill Owen's dead.'

King sat stunned. 'What?' he said after a moment.

'A coronary. It happened this morning. Look, you'd better see this.' He handed King a carefully handwritten sheet of paper. 'It's a note to the top brass.'

King took it and read it.

Dear Commissioner,

For some time I have been working very hard, and have been depressed by lack of advancement in the Force and the fact that my wife has been disappointed in me. I have also been very much in love with the wife of Mr Harry King, though I trust I hid my feelings. Recently, however, and thanks to certain narcotics which I am ashamed to say I have been in the habit of taking, I have been horrified by the knowledge that Mrs King was not what I had

*thought. I first suspected it at a picnic when I
thought I saw little snakes round her head, and my
wife Madge said that I once called out Medusa in
my sleep. She thought it was another woman, but
Medusa was, of course, the chief Gorgon, as you will
be aware, sir, with snakes instead of hair. I have been
thinking about it ever since I killed her, which I had
to do, as you will understand. I could not let my good
friend Harry King go on being married to Medusa,
if she was Medusa, nor could I go on living without
her if she was not, but I think she was, and so, sir*

There was no more; only a squiggly line going down
the page and petering out.

'Rambling, of course,' said Harper. 'He was struck
down before he'd finished. Tragic. I had a very difficult
session with Madge Owen. She kept saying, "I could
get you for this. Overworked! I could get you for
this. " '

It was not Harry King's day. He sat there speechless,
grey and motionless, until there was a knock at the
door. Alice Caldwell walked in, looking fresh and clean
and smart in her police uniform.

King stared at her for fully half a minute – letting it
sink in, thinking about the deadly parapet he had been
walking. The two of them watched him, until finally
he had to say something.

'Dicker?'

'The suitcases were made of processed heroin,
varnished over. Apart from the metal parts. They went
to the man they called Tom to be rendered down and
converted into tablets. They've been trying it with

opium, too, but there are difficulties because opium gets sticky. It's a problem for us you know. Short of cutting pieces off everyone's luggage, it's hard to see what to do. Awkward.'

'Not as awkward as being mauled by Dicker,' Alice Caldwell said sharply and unexpectedly.

'Alice got the Sure Friendship job when we heard that Dicker was after the firm,' Harper went on. 'Then she let him pick her up, and gained his confidence with bits of information.'

'Easy, really,' added Alice. 'Except for being periodically eaten alive by a baboon. And the jewellery wasn't even real. Still, as he didn't get what he really wanted from me. . . .' She paused, then said, 'Though I must say it was touch and go sometimes. Like phoning you after I'd given that last suitcase to Tom. I thought I'd never get through to you, sir,' she finished reproachfully.

Then she excused herself from the room.

'I did a deal with Alf Bauer,' said Harper when she had gone. 'Dicker won't be charged with murder. He's pleaded guilty to manslaughter, plus most of the drugs charges. The combined stretch in prison will amount to about the same as what they call "life". It'll save us some bother.'

King nodded mechanically.

'But I have got a bit of insurance,' Harper continued. 'Just in case he changes his mind.' He picked up a tape cassette from his desk, let King see it, and replaced it. 'The tape from the Wargrove Hotel. You're on it, too.'

Harry King stared at it. Then he said, 'Tape or no tape, you could have picked Buller up before he was killed. Tape or no tape, you could have turned him in.'

Harper said: 'He might have changed his plans, mightn't he? He had to be followed to the end. It was operationally necessary.'

There was another silence. Harper stood up. More slowly, King did likewise.

Harper held out his hand. 'Buller was a dangerous animal,' he said, 'and our prisons are overcrowded.'

Harry King nodded woodenly once more. 'Yes,' he said, but he was thinking that the animals behind prison bars are gentle and tame compared to those that roam the human mind.

The two men shook hands: Harper firmly, King listlessly. Then the pallid fox, head bowed, turned and left the room.

Author's Note

All characters and incidents in this book are fictitious. However, I have reason to believe that the so-called suitcases which are described, and the way they are used, may be authentic. J.B.